THE
Unicorn
DESTINY

Ginger Summers

Gotham Books

30 N Gould St.
Ste. 20820, Sheridan, WY 82801
https://gothambooksinc.com/

Phone: 1 (307) 464-7800

© 2023 *Ginger Summers*. All rights reserved.

No part of this book may be reproduced, stored in a retrieval system, or transmitted by any means without the written permission of the author.

Published by Gotham Books (November 25, 2023)

ISBN: 979-8-88775-457-4 (P)
ISBN: 979-8-88775-458-1 (E)

Because of the dynamic nature of the Internet, any web addresses or links contained in this book may have changed since publication and may no longer be valid.

The views expressed in this work are solely those of the author and do not necessarily reflect the views of the publisher, and the publisher hereby disclaims any responsibility for them.

Character List Unicorn Destiny

Colorado

Cynthia Ann Hanson (Cindy) - Best friends with Gia and Katrina.
Alexander McCullum Hanson (Alex) - Father of Cindy and Aaron.
Sandra Murphy Hanson (Sandy) - Mother of Cindy and Aaron.
Aaron Maxwell Hanson - Lost son of Alex and Sandy.
Katrina Lynn O' Connor - Friend of Cindy and Gia.
Georgia Amanda Branson (Gia) - Friend of Cindy and Gia.

Land of the Unicorns

Knight - Leader of Starlight Tribe.
Star - Mother of Lunar and Starscape.
Charger (Lunar) - Son of Knight and Star
Leader of the last unicorn tribe – Father of Amethyst and Obsidian.
Starscape - Twin brother of Lunar.
Moonbeam - Mother to Amethyst and Obsidian; Co-leader of the last unicorn tribe.
Obsidian - Son of Lunar and Moonbeam; twin of Amethyst.
Amethyst - Daughter of Lunar and Moonbeam; twin of Obsidian.
Omon - Juvenile Dragon; Guardian of the last unicorn herd.
The Hunter - Hideous creature that hunts unicorns.
Uniscale - Bond servant to The Hunter.

Chapter 1

Alarms and sirens blared, breaking through the quiet night.

"Evacuate! Evacuate! Fire less than five miles away from this area."

"Cindy! Wake up! The wildfire is just a few miles away! Wake up, wake up!" Sandy said as she shook her daughter from a sound sleep. "Quickly, grab your things. The wind shifted and broke through the fire lines. It's coming our way now, and we need to go right now!

Get your stuff fast! We need to get to the car immediately!"

Stumbling around her room in a confused rush, Cindy grabbed the last of her clothes, stuffing them into her backpack as she crossed the room, giving it a quick scan. She ran back to her bed and grabbed her stuffed unicorn and the diary that she had received last year for Christmas. As she picked up her diary, she noticed the shiny chain with the unicorn charm on it she hadn't seen for awhile. She grabbed it and was grateful she had seen it, knowing how important it was to her mother because of the stories her mother had told her about her brother's imaginary adventures into a magical land that he claimed the charm had brought him.

When she reached to pick it up, she felt it tingle in her hand. Not sure what to think, she put it in her pocket. With one last quick check around the room, she looked at the top of her desk. She saw the bowling trophies she had from when she was on the Youth Classic bowling team at her local bowling alley. She also saw the medals she had won from track last year. She wanted so much to grab a trophy or medal, but she didn't have room in her pack for anything else. She really wanted to but couldn't carry anything more.

Cindy's mother ran to the file cabinet grabbing the folder with the important papers. She flipped through their wedding license, birth certificates, medical records and passports. When she came across her first child's death certificate tears sprang to her eyes. She stopped and drifted off in thought. Cindy hurried over to her mom and gave her a hug knowing she was thinking about the loss of her brother, but she knew they needed to get moving.

"Mom we need to get going, I can feel the heat approaching through the walls"

Cindy pulled her mother's arms and got her mom to move and continue to head to the car. There were also tears in Cindy's eyes.

"I have got to grab the albums from the shelves and the pictures from the walls," Sandy said.

With the last dash to save the albums from the bookshelf across the living room, Cindy turned just in time to see her mother's misstep, but saw her mom recover. She heard her mom say, "Ouch," but Sandy hobbled back to gather as many of the albums and pictures that she could.

Cindy ran toward the car. She tossed her pack and things into the back seat. Then she heard Molly whining.

"I need to get Molly," Cindy said.

"We haven't got time," her father, Alexander, said. When Cindy tried to open the door, he said, "No, you need to stay in the car."

"I am not going to abandon her. She would never abandon me." She opened the car door and jumped out. She ran back to the house and called out to the cocker spaniel. She heard whimpering but didn't know where it was coming from. She ran to the living room searching under and around the furniture, calling again for Molly as she felt the intense heat building around her with smoke rushing like rain into the house. She heard glass breaking and saw flames scrambling in like unwanted guests as the windows crashed and broke. Crawling on the ground to keep from choking on the heavy smoke, she continued searching for Molly, now moving into the kitchen. Suddenly, she heard a loud bark over the sound of the fire which seemed to reach its fingers toward the kitchen window. Looking under the table, she saw Molly had made herself as small as possible in the far corner under the table. Grabbing the chairs and throwing them across the room, Cindy was able to grab the terrified dog's collar and pull her out.

Cindy sprinted into the living room, as her mother ran into the house again. Ignoring the pain from her twisted ankle, she headed toward her daughter. Cindy looked out the glass back door and saw a landslide of critters running from the woods straight for the sliding door. Everything was trying to escape the fire.

Quickly, she opened the door, so the animals wouldn't crash into the glass while she was pulling on Molly's collar. With the renewed oxygen available, the fire gushed in through the opened door.

Molly wouldn't move. She was petrified and burned by the embers of fire landing on her fur. Picking up the terrified twenty pound cocker spaniel who squirmed in her arms, Cindy ran toward her mother, who was approaching from the direction of the front of the house. Molly broke from Cindy's arms, and her mother scooped the terrified dog up and turned toward the car thinking that Cindy was right behind her. The sudden loss of extra weight caused Cindy to lose her balance, and she fell to her hands and knees, her arms stinging from the fire that rushed in through the glass door. Alexander raced to grab her just as her favorite climbing tree fell onto the roof of the house. Hearing the terrible crash, Cindy turned to see the fire jump from the tree, and the house erupt into flames as the fire greedily ate the shingles of the roof, devouring their home and all that was left inside.

Cindy ran past her mother and opened the back door. Molly jumped in and Sandy climbed painfully into the front seat. Alexander dashed around the back of the SUV, slamming the trunk as he passed on his way to the driver's side. Everyone quickly fastened their seatbelts and gravel spewed from behind the SUV as Alexander turned the car to head down the long driveway to the main road.

On either side of the road, a menacing glow of fire attacked the trees, mercilessly charring the once beautiful limbs until they were as black as night. As they drove down the road, Cindy hugged Molly tightly as Molly whined. Cindy could hear the ear-piercing shriek of the trees being engulfed and knew that Molly was still panicked. With burning embers pelting the vehicle, they sped down the road to safety with flames racing them, just missing the SUV. A stream of animals poured out of the woods, half charred and dying and falling as flames greedily attacked everything in its path. The air filled with flying insects, and birds darkened the sky, as dusty gray orange clouds consumed any starlight and changed the sky to black tar. Ash and smoke stung everyone's eyes and parched throats as the fire turned feral. Cindy held the charm in her hand and remembered the stories her mother had told her about Aaron.

Chapter 2

It was more than two hours before they were able to follow the taillights from the mass of cars off the mountain. They passed through the town that welcomed them for the duration of the fire. Arriving at the hotel reserved for evacuees, Cindy and her family exited the car with medics quickly examining them to make sure they were not hurt or experiencing smoke inhalation. They were given an apple and a granola bar to eat, and water to drink. By the time they got to the medics, Sandy's ankle was swollen to the size of a softball. They checked her ankle and wrapped it with an ace bandage to help support it. They told her when she got to her room to ice her ankle and to stay off of it for a day.

The medics also wanted to check Cindy's arms to make sure the burns from the fire weren't serious. Grateful that she had been wearing her flame-resistant long sleeve pajama top that fit snugly around her arms, the burns she received from the fire were just first degree like she had been sunburned. Molly was checked over by a vet, who treated her singed body and put cream on her skin to soothe the pain. They were given keys and directions to which room they would be assigned until it was safe to return to their home. They headed to their room with Sandy leaning heavily on Alexander as he helped her walk to the room. Cindy was moping behind with her head down and feeling miserable as the guilt crept in because she felt responsible about the fire devouring their home. She continued to walk up to their room, looked around and bemoaned the fact that they didn't have a home. Even though they were at a hotel, it wouldn't be fun. It wasn't like they were on a vacation. She had no idea what had become of her friends. She hoped they were safe but living in different areas. It was hard to know if they had been displaced also.

Sandy hugged Cindy, "Thank heavens you are safe! I thought we lost you to the flames, you crazy girl."

"You were brave, but also foolish to go back to get Molly. How are your legs? You fell hard to the ground when Molly jumped out of your arms," Alexander said.

Cindy hugged both her parents. "They seem to be a bit bruised and skinned, but I am fine. The worst part is that my arms are still stinging from the fire when I opened the glass door. The medics gave me some Aloe Vera gel to put on my arms to cool the sting."

"Well, I guess we had better get settled into this place. We may be here for a while," Sandy said.

"I'm glad that the room has a kitchenette, so we can do some of our own cooking," Alexander said.

"But it's still not a kitchen. It only has a microwave and a toaster oven, no real oven or dishwasher. I wouldn't call it being able to cook our own meals. We can only eat a bunch of microwaveable meals," said Cindy.

"Now Cindy, it's not that bad. Besides, we can get a mini crockpot from the store, and then we can have fresh meals. There are some really good microwave meals available," said Sandy.

"And it will be good for you to wash your dishes by hand. Aaron actually liked helping to wash dishes," Alexander said.

Thanks Dad. Of course, you'd have to compare me to Aaron. Will this ever change? Will Dad ever be able to move on with life and stop bringing my brother up when I say or do something that Aaron would have done better?

After her dad helped Sandy into a chair to rest and put her ankle up, he went back to the car and unloaded what they had managed to save from their home. He set about organizing their temporary "home."

Cindy moved over to the bed next to her mom by the window and gazed out at the sky. In the distance, she could see the black clouds of ash and smoke swallowing up the sunrise. Molly jumped onto the bed and curled up next to Cindy.

"I am sorry that the wind changed so quickly, and we had to leave our home. I wish we would have paid more attention to the movement of the fire. I really wish we would have had more things packed before we had to escape from it," Sandy said.

"What really matters is that our whole family is together, and we are alive. I think one of the scariest things for me was the thought of not having Molly," Cindy said as she patted the exhausted dog.

"I am very proud of you for getting Molly. She is such a special dog. Your brother Aaron picked her out when she was a puppy."

"I am so sorry that I opened the glass doors. I should have remembered oxygen fuels the fire. I never should have opened that door. I hated to see the animals crash into the glass, but they still got devoured by the flames as well as our home." Cindy could not hold back the tears any longer as they burst from her eyes.

"My brave sweet girl. Don't blame yourself for the loss of our home. I would have done the same thing at your age. You have such a tender heart. You are always putting others before yourself."

Snuggling close to her mom, both had tears pouring out of their eyes. For a brief moment the tears slowed down and then a new burst of tears exploded from Cindy's eyes when she thought about her friends and if they were safe.

"What is it my girl? What are you thinking about? "Sandy asked.

Sniffling, she said, "I hope my friends are safe. I hope I will be able to see them again. I wonder how Gia and her mom are doing. I hope they're okay. I wonder if Katrina and her family got out safely."

Walking over to Cindy and her mom, Alexander set a hand on her shoulder saying, "I am sure they are all safe, I will see if I can find anything out," Alexander said.

After their cry fest, their noses were assaulted with the gross smell of the smoke on their bodies and hair.

"Wow! I stink! I need to shower and get this sickening smell off me," Cindy said.

"Yes, I do too, but I will need some help from you after you're done with your shower." Alexander said,

"You both stink. Why don't I run to the store and get some supplies for our stay and you guys get cleaned up. I'll be back soon. Anything special either of you want?" Cindy said,

"Can you get some orange dark chocolate and some potato chips?" Sandy added,

"How about some Tylenol and laundry detergent?" Alexander smiled at the two people he loved most in the world and said, "Righto," before he left.

Once Cindy came out of the shower, she was reminded again how she was not at home, how the water pressure was low, and how she had to hop out of the shower to get the shampoo and soap the hotel provided for them, as well as the small, scratchy, stiff, bleached towels that barely fit around her as she dried off her body.

After Cindy was dressed again, she helped her mom get cleaned up. She helped her mother get resituated in the chair with her leg elevated. Then she found the ice machine and filled a bag from the mostly empty machine for her mother's ankle.

With her mom settled, Cindy began to pace the floor back and forth, not knowing what to do. She turned on the TV, flipping through the channels, but all she saw were the terrible reports about the fire, continually showing the firefighters fighting the fire, the people being evacuated from their homes, interviews with people who were being evacuated. She watched for her friends but didn't recognize any of the people who were talking. She got more and more anxious about her friends, wondering if they were okay.

Turn off the TV, Cindy," her mom said,

"What can I do? I have nothing, nothing at all. My books are burned, my treasured items are all gone. I have nothing to do. I have lost my whole life, nothing will ever be the same!"

Sandy sat up straighter in the chair. "Cynthia Lynn, lower your voice! Sit down right now."

Cindy went to the bed and plopped on the side with her arms folded and her eyes cast down toward the floor.

Sandy continued in a loud whisper, "Look at me please." When her daughter raised her eyes, she said, "I know you're scared and worried about your friends. I am, too. I know that you're sad about losing the house and your things in it. I am, too. I also know that you're sleep deprived. I am, too. However, dwelling on the negative is not going to change a thing. We need to make the best of this situation. Let's take a look at the positive for a minute. No one in our family has died. Yes, our house is gone, but that's only things, and we have insurance to replace them. Yes, I know that there were many memories in those things, and that's unfortunate, but we can make new memories. The important thing is we are all still together and other than a few singed hairs and a sprained ankle, we're lucky to have this room, even if it only has a microwave. If we don't want to cook, there is free food being prepared for us by all kinds of people all over the area. We're very lucky, and it's time we ALL appreciate it."

Cindy looked at her mom. "I'm sorry. You're right about all of it. I'm just scared," she said in a whimper, lowering her head.

Sandy said, "I understand, but I'm pretty sure our temporary neighbors would appreciate it if we didn't introduce ourselves through the walls."

Cindy smiled and said, "I'll introduce myself in the morning and apologize." Then she got up and hugged her mom.

Cindy's phone rang. Looking at the ID, she saw it was her best friend, Gia, and quickly answered the call.

"Gia! I am so glad to hear from you. I was terrified something bad had happened to you!

Are you alright?"

"I'm fine. My mom and I just arrived at the hotel."

"What hotel are you at?"

"We are at The Landing Inn."

"We are, too!"

"It was so scary seeing the flames devour the forest a little ways from us, and then we had to be rushed out of our apartment by firefighters. We hardly had time to grab anything."

"Yes, I almost got burnt to a crisp. I had to find Molly before we could leave. I heard her crying. I just had to save her. I finally found her in the kitchen, hiding under the table. Just after I left the house and got several feet away, the roof caught fire," Cindy said.

Gia mumbled something, then added to Cindy, "I need to go. The medics are approaching us. I'll call you back soon and let you know what room we'll be in."

"Great! Bye! That was Gia and her mom. They just arrived at the hotel. It sounds like they even had less time than we did to evacuate their apartment."

"Oh no! I am glad they are safe," Sandy said.

"Hey Cindy, guess who I saw at the store? Katrina and her dad! They are staying on the fifth floor in room 520," her father said as he walked in the door, his arms laden with grocery bags.

"Wow, that's great! I just got off the phone with Gia... She and her mom just got here fifteen minutes ago."

"I am so happy your friends are here and safe. This fire is the worst I've ever seen. I heard it has consumed more than 200,000 acres of land," Alexander said.

"Wow, this fire is huge! I am so glad to have my friends to hang out with. I should give Katrina a call."

Just as Cindy was getting ready to call Katrina, her phone buzzed.

"Hi Katrina. I was just about to call you; my dad just said he saw you at the store."

"I wanted to invite you up to my room to hang out."

"Did you know Gia and her mom are also here?" Cindy asked.

"No, when did they get here?"

"I guess they got here about an hour ago. She called me just as the medics were getting ready to see that they were ok. I'll give you a call when Gia gets checked in, and we can come up together. Anyway, Dad just bought a boatload of groceries, and I need to help put things away since Mom hurt her ankle. I'll tell you about it when I see you. I'll need to take Molly out for a walk. Do you want to come too? That way we can all talk."

"Sure! That sounds like a great idea. See you soon."

Chapter 3

The three girls hugged each other when they met in the lobby later that morning.

"I'm so glad to see you guys!" Cindy said. "I'm glad we're all at the same hotel."

"I was so scared when the loudspeaker sounded, telling us to leave our home immediately.

I just barely had time to grab my unicorn pillow and some clothes," Gia said.

"My parents told me a couple days ago to pack an evacuation bag. My dad had overheard others in our area talking about a voluntary move from our area," Katrina said. Then she added quietly, "Don't eat the food here. It's awful. We had breakfast yesterday, and the eggs tasted like rubber. We have good food up in our suite. Why don't you guys come up there, and we can make panini sandwiches and melon balls. We also have sherbet for dessert. Does that sound okay?"

Cindy looked at Gia. "I'm okay with that. In our kitchenette, we have canned soup and instant hot chocolate."

Gia said, "I would have been fine with sandwiches in the common room. What is a panini?"

Gia said, "I spent the summer working on my aunt's farm. I delivered three colts and learned about how to make natural tonics to help them feel better. I'll try a panini."

The girls headed up to Katrina's room.

Cindy and Gia were a little jealous because Katrina's parents had prepared well. The room looked as if the family had been planning this as a holiday trip for a long time. Katrina had several books, movies, games--

even her laptop computer and her video game station were set up on the desk. Gia and Cindy were envious of what Katrina had but Katrina always had more.

"Wow, this is fancier than my real house," said Cindy. "The one that is totally burned down."

"Yeah, but you can rebuild yours. Everything I had is totally gone," Gia said quietly with a start of a tear coming from her eye.

Cindy reached over and gave her friend a hug. "We'll get through this together. You and your mom can always stay with us, wherever we are."

"We'll see what happens. There's always my aunt's farm. We don't have to worry about it now. Right now, let's go find out what a panini is," Gia said, trying to lighten the mood. Then when they went into the kitchen, she raised her voice and added, "Wow Katrina! It looks like you are set up for a vacation."

Cindy said, "How lucky for you that your parents had time to pack before leaving."

"Why didn't you guys leave when you heard about the fire? It's been all over the news?"

Katrina said as she opened the lid on the panini press, took out the sandwich, placed it on a plate with melon on the side and handed it to Gia

Gia looked down at the Italian sandwich and said, "So that's a panini!" before taking a big bite!

"We had been watching 9 News before we headed to bed and according to the news, our home was safe, but then after I had gone to sleep a strong wind came up and changed directions at about one this morning. Mom woke me up and told me to quickly grab my backpack and fill it with clothes. As I left the room, I took a quick look around and grabbed the unicorn necklace my mom gave me a few years ago." said Cindy.

Katrina handed her a plate with a panini and fruit. Cindy dug right in. "At least you had time to grab things. My mom had just gotten done with a twelve hour shift at a nursing home. I was just getting ready to get in my PJs when we heard a pounding on the door, and a firefighter told us to leave immediately. I was just able to grab my compass and my pocket knife from my night stand, and I also grabbed my stuffed unicorn from my bed that my dad gave me before he left my mom," said Gia.

"Wow! How scary it must have been! "said Katrina, as she pulled the last sandwich from the machine.

Suddenly, Cindy felt a tingling sensation from the unicorn charm and brought it out and looked at it. As she fingered it, she started to remember the horror of the monstrous fire devouring her home; she couldn't stop the tears from coming as she realized they had lost everything. She didn't even have a home to return to; all of her possessions were gone too. *What were they going to do? Where would her family live? Would they have to move somewhere else? Would she have to start a new life in an entirely different place than what she is familiar with? Would she have to change schools next fall?*

Gia came over with her empty plate and realized that Cindy was in tears. Setting her plate down, she wrapped Cindy in her arms. Not needing to know why Cindy was crying, soon Gia was crying also. As she was wrapping her arms around Cindy, she felt a sharp sting.

"Ouch! I felt like I got pricked with a pin. No, I just got poked by the horn on the unicorn charm" she said as Cindy pulled the charm out of her pocket.

Both Cindy and Gia looked down at the charm. A sharp tingle hit both girls at the same time and they jumped at the sensation of icy hot energy flowing from the charm.

The black unicorn started to shimmer with the golden horn becoming more golden as they looked at it. Cindy felt a cool breeze dusting her hair like the coolness of fall.

"Do you feel a gentle breeze flowing in your hair, Gia?"

"Yes, it's weird. I don't think any windows are open in here; besides if they were, we would feel the stifling heat of the sun coming in through the windows not a cool breeze," Gia said.

"Does the charm look brighter to you? Is it just the reflection from the window or are my eyes just playing tricks on me?" Cindy asked.

"It seems to have a prism of light reflecting off the obsidian unicorn. I see a rainbow of colors dancing on the ceiling."

Running over to Cindy and Gia, Katrina said, "You are glowing! A ring of light is encircling you two. What are you doing? Where did the shimmer come from?"

Molly followed behind Katrina as she walked toward Cindy and Gia. "You look like you are encased in a giant bubble like when we were little kids, and we would make the monster bubbles with the big wands that we would move over our whole bodies."

She reached through the shimmering encasement and found she couldn't pull her hand back out. Instead, it moved toward Cindy's chain as if she was trying to pull the chain away from Gia and Cindy. Molly growled and tried to snap at the bubble, but it wouldn't pop, and it wouldn't allow her to enter either.

"I didn't pinch you. Are you sure it wasn't the horn of the unicorn charm? I know when I reached in my pocket I felt like I got poked with the horn, but then I felt an icy tingling as I pulled the necklace out of my pocket," Cindy told Gia.

Suddenly Katrina was sucked inside the bubble with Gia and Cindy.

"What kind of trick are you playing on me? First, it feels like you are pinching me; then I feel a strong pull into the bubble, and now, everything seems to be blurring and fading away. I am wanting to get out of this thing, but I can't. I feel like the time I fell so hard off the high balance beam that I got the air knocked out of me in gymnastics class."

"Molly! Molly, where is Molly? I barely hear her barking, and I only see a cloudy blur of her. Oh no, I can't leave her again." Cindy pounded on the glass-like ball that formed around them.

As the ring of light continued to encircle the girls, peace overtook them, and they all started to relax. They felt a swirling breeze and saw a pinpoint of plasma form in the center of the ball. It caused their hair to frizz out and pulled Gia's braid straight up. They heard a snapping flame encircle the outside of the glass ball. Grasping hands, they held tightly to each other, afraid they would slide apart as light surrounded them. Then a sudden gust of wind picked the ball up, and they felt themselves falling like they were on a long steep roller coaster slope where they felt their stomachs drop. They coasted down a slide with rainbow colors encircling them. As they dropped deeper and deeper into nothingness, they saw flashes of white pass in front of their eyes as if the white was running from something terrifying. They heard hoof beats crunching over dried leaves then felt heat blaze their skin.

One of the white flashes separated Gia from the clasp of Katrina and Cindy's hand; as the flash went by, Gia thought she felt silky fur pass over her hands and under her rump. She found herself falling out of control, and she landed on the ground and rolled into a massive prickly bush.

Chapter 4

Cindy looked around the forest where she had landed. The scent of rich old wood was thick in the air. Tilting her neck back, she glanced higher and higher, until she was staring at the very top of some of the tallest trees she had ever seen. She and her parents had visited the Sequoia Forest last year, and these trees were bigger than even some of those. The ferns beneath her feet were so thick that her feet bounced when she took a step. Moving toward Gia, who was on the ground, Cindy marveled at the sunlight that played between the trunks of the huge trees.

Katrina reached into her pocket as she gasped for air and took a deep breath from her inhaler, grateful as the medicine quieted her imminent asthma attack. She, too, looked around and saw that Gia was sitting in the undergrowth beside a large tree. She didn't spend much time outside in the wilderness but was pretty sure that she was no longer in Colorado. None of these trees were near their home, and there were so many ferns. Mom had some of this type of fern. She called them Boston ferns, but her plants looked tiny compared to the huge fronds she saw on these plants. One was nearly as tall as she was. She started to feel like she was in a movie where the dad's experiment went haywire, and now she was stuck in some wild habitat. She, too, started moving toward Gia.

"Are you okay, Katrina?" Cindy said as she reached her.

"Yes. I just need to continue to take deep breaths as my lungs open back up," she said as she looked around her. She took a second puff when she saw trees towering above her.

She felt like a mouse. "Where are we?"

As Katrina looked around, she panicked even more. She had never been in "the wild." She was frightened but didn't want her friends to know. She sat down behind a rock and started to cry and rock back and forth until she was able to settle her nerves.

Suddenly, Gia called out. "Ow! What is that pricking me?" Gia shouted as she jumped up from the ground.

"It looks like you landed on a prickly pear," Cindy said.

Gia moaned, "Owwww! It's a good thing I'm wearing jeans. I don't like these things poking me. Can you guys help me pick these spines out of my jeans?"

Cindy said, "Sure. Turn around, so I can see your pants in the light." When Gia complied, Cindy added, "Whoa! You hit the jackpot! There must be 100 spines in your jeans!" She began helping her friend.

Gia said sardonically, "Tell me about it."

"Cindy, how did you land on your feet?" Gia asked, rubbing her leg where the spines had poked her.

"I don't know. I came down the slide just as fast as you all did."

"Let's get serious. Where are we, and how did we get here?" Gia asked.

"It must have been the unicorn charm my mom gave me a while back. I remember her telling me a story about how my brother, Aaron, loved the charm. He claimed it was magic, and he was able to travel to a land full of unicorns. He even claimed he could talk to them. She said he had a grand imagination."

"Wow! It would be neat to have a unicorn you could talk to," Katrina said, coming from behind the rock. "I would be happy to just see a real live unicorn," said Gia.

"I sure hope we will be able to get back to the hotel. This air is stifling," Katrina said.

Cindy looked at Katrina and said, "Yeah, that's the most important thing to think about right now. *The air is stifling!* Have you noticed that the trees in this forest are over 100 feet tall? They're silver green. They don't look anything like the ones we have at home. They're more like sequoias, but not really."

Katrina shot back. "Sure Cindy. You would know what a sequoia looks like. You know everything. Since you DO know everything, please tell me how we got here. It was your charm that sent us to this godforsaken spot."

"My charm! No one asked you to grab hold of it!"

"I thought I was saving my friends, what I thought were my two best friends, from...well I don't know from what. I just know that I thought I was saving my two best friends from something and wanted to be with you two!"

Gia, who had been watching her two best friends argue, decided it was time to step in. "Stop it, you two. We're here. We're together. We're all we've got! We've been in situations like this before...well actually, we haven't been in a situation like this before, but we've solved problems. Remember when we became lost at the Unicorn Festival in Littleton?"

Cindy and Katrina looked at Gia who hardly ever raised her voice at anyone and who was practically yelling now. Then they looked at each other. Then they started laughing. Gia was right. They did do better when they worked as a team.

Cindy apologized first. "Sorry Katrina. I didn't mean to be so sarcastic. When I get scared, I don't always think of others and I become rude. Will you accept my apology?"

Katrina hugged Cindy. "Of course, I will. I was rude too. I shouldn't have thought of myself. I'm scared too. I have no idea where we are, and I am hot, but that is no excuse for being rude. Will you accept my apology?" she said with a grin.

Cindy smiled, "Of course! We're best buds."

Gia, always the practical one, said, "I am sure we can find our way back up whatever that was, but until then, we need to remember exactly where we landed, so we don't lose our way.

"I can tie my ribbon to this sapling, so we will be able to know this is where we landed," Katrina said.

"That might be a good idea; however, it might be easier to recognize a group of trees since they're so big. What about those two trees growing together that cross at the top? They kind of look like the end of a slide," Gia said.

Cindy and Katrina thought that was a good idea, and Katrina tied her ribbon to a sapling by the two trees.

"I hope we will be able to find water and food in this place if we end up being here for a while," Gia added.

"Look at all these trees. They're as tall as redwood trees! Where are we?" Cindy asked.

"I believe we are in an ancient forest." Gia took a deep breath, trying to breathe in the fresh scent of the trees. Then she asked, "Do you guys smell the scent of charred grass? I bet there's a valley nearby that has been burned," said Gia. "I wonder if there was a lightning storm? Remember how that forest fire started last summer when lightning struck that old dry tree?"

"I hope we can get out of these woods and back to the hotel. That was a hard landing onto the forest floor," Katrina complained, rubbing her backside.

Gia and Cindy just glanced at each other and shook their heads.

Looking around under the trees, they took inventory of their new surroundings, paying close attention to the details of what landmarks were around. The girls were surrounded by trees the size of redwoods, and they couldn't even put their arms around the trunks of the trees if they joined hands. At the bottom of the trees, there were huge ferns nearly as tall as the girls. When they looked around, they were reminded of the pictures they had seen of the redwood forest in California, and as they looked further, it almost seemed they were in a big basin where a fire had burned, but most of the trees had been spared.

Gia agreed with Katrina, "I agree. We need to get home. This place is too weird, and our parents will be worried about us." She looked around her. "How do we do that?" The three girls stared at each other.

Then Cindy said, "Well, it started when we all held onto the charm. Let's try that."

She held out the charm, and then, Gia put her hand on top of it. There was no glowing or shimmering.

Cindy said, "Maybe we need all three of us together again. Come on Katrina."

Katrina took a deep breath and walked over to her friends. She reached down and grabbed the chain and closed her eyes. Nothing happened. The girls waited. Katrina opened her eyes. Still, nothing happened.

Katrina said, "Well, now what?"

Cindy looked around the clearing where they stood and suddenly saw a light shining from within a tree. "Look at that tree. It has a light inside of it," she said.

Chapter 5

Gia and Katrina looked where Cindy pointed. All they saw was a tree that seemed like a cave. Cindy started walking toward the tree.

Gia called to her, "Hey Cindy, I thought we were going to try to go home. I'm pretty sure we didn't come that way. Let's go back this way," pointing back the way they had come.

Cindy turned back to the two girls. "Can't you see that light shining through that tree? I think we should explore it. This whole thing is so weird. Maybe this way is the way home. What do you guys think?"

Katrina stared at the tree. "I don't see any light in that tree. Do you, Gia?"

Gia said, "I don't see anything but a big black hole. Cindy, come on back here, so we can talk about it. I think it's important that whatever we decide to do, we stay together."

On her way back to the other two, Cindy said, "I agree, but I really think this might be the way out. You guys really can't see it? Maybe I can just take a quick peek."

Gia interrupted, "No way! We're all in this together. If something happens to you, how are we going to get home? I don't know how we're supposed to get back, but I feel certain that we need to stay together. What do you think, Katrina?"

Katrina looked between the two girls and put her hands on her hips. "Now you ask my opinion? You didn't when you grabbed hold of the unicorn charm. I want to go back to the hotel. I was happy, or as happy as I could be without being home, at the hotel. I don't want to be here!" she added, stamping her foot.

Gia and Cindy now looked at each other, surprised at their friend's outburst.

Then Gia said, "We tried going back by holding onto the charm. That didn't work. Standing here in this...," she looked around at the amazing forest in which they found themselves, "...unusual land, doesn't appear to be getting us back to the hotel, but the one thing that I do feel strongly about is that we need to stay together."

Katrina sighed, "You just asked my opinion, and now you're ignoring me."

It was now Cindy's turn to sigh. "Okay Katrina. I want to go home too. My mom is hurt, and I'm sure all of our parents are worried about us. I'm also worried about Molly. We left her alone in your suite. She probably needs to go out again, and she's probably hungry and thirsty. So, how do you see us getting home?"

Katrina said, "I don't know."

Cindy said, "So, if standing here is not working, how about if we explore the tree? If we don't see anything that helps us, then we can come back and try another way. What do you say?"

Katrina looked at the ground and said, "Fine."

Gia shook her head slightly while looking at Cindy and said, "Okay, let's give it a try."

Cindy turned back toward the tree with Gia and Katrina following. As they looked deeper into the cave-like doorway, and they followed her through the tree, they came upon a beautiful Turquoise River and heard the rush of water streaming over the rocks. Their eyes were surprised by the sunlight dancing across the water with a sparkling of purple stones catching the sunlight. Gia and Katrina continued following Cindy along a well worn path on the other side of the cave-like tree toward a valley. It was like she knew exactly where they were going. The girls were greeted with the horrid, acrid smell of charred wood and grass. In the distance, Cindy pointed toward a huge valley that was totally black, but in the center, there seemed to be a white patch surrounded by charred trees.

"Look at that weird section of land," Cindy said pointing toward the patch of white. "It looks like a valley that has been burnt, but I'm not sure why there would be white in the middle of it," Gia said.

"Let's get a closer look," Cindy said, quickly moving forward in the direction of the site.

Katrina looked back from where they had come. "Wait! Wait! Look behind us! I thought we were keeping track of where we were going, but all I see is an endless stream of green ferns blocking the view from where we came. I can't even see the tree we went through."

"Oh, no!" Gia said, looking back.

Cindy stopped at Gia's voice. As both Cindy and Gia looked back at Katrina, they realized no one had remembered to keep track of where they walked. Cindy's curiosity had gotten her into trouble once again.

"Shoot! You're right, Katrina," Cindy said.

"What are we going to do now?" Katrina whimpered.

"Cindy, shouldn't we try to find a way back to our families? They have lost so much, why should we add to the pain by going off on an adventure?" Gia said.

"I want to find our way back to the tree. I don't want to go on this adventure. I want to go home!" whined Katrina. She started wheezing again, turning back toward the way they had come.

"I want to check out the valley first and find out what the white is in the middle of the burnt area," Cindy said as her charm around her neck started to glow. "Whoa! My charm is glowing! It's pulling me toward the valley. I hear a cry for help. I need to help them! I can't resist the pull," said Cindy as she headed toward the valley.

"Come on, Katrina. We need to follow Cindy," said Gia.

Grabbing her by the arm, Gia pulled Katrina to get her moving. "Do you want to stay here by yourself or follow Cindy? She is the one who has the magic charm, and her charm is most likely our way back to our world. Besides, she said her charm was glowing, so maybe this is the way back to our world," Gia said firmly.

Cindy heard the voices of her friends growing fainter. She stopped and saw them at the top of the hill. She hadn't even noticed that she had been running. Torn between wanting to wait for her friends to catch up or going into the valley, she panicked. She desperately wanted to wait for her friends.

She cried out in a hurry, "I need to keep moving!"

With every step she took, she left a path of golden flowers, as she moved forward. All the heaviness of grief started to leave her. All she focused on was the pull and the anticipation of a grand adventure where she could leave hurt and pain behind.

The girls saw her just long enough to see the direction she was going, and then they lost sight of her completely.

"Slow down," said Katrina. "I can't keep up." She leaned forward to catch her breath.

"But I can barely see where Cindy is going, and it is getting harder to see the valley where she is headed," said Gia.

"Look! I can see a golden glow," said Katrina pointing in the direction where Cindy had gone. "I barely see Cindy's form, but it seems the trail is being blazed for us to follow. Let's slow down a little."

"Okay, we can slow down a little, but I do want to catch up with her soon. I don't want to become separated. How is your asthma doing now?" Gia asked, torn between wanting to follow Cindy and needing to make sure Katrina's attack was resolving.

Katrina said, "Chill out! We can just follow that glow on the path where she's gone."

Gia turned to Katrina, "Are you alright? There's nothing there."

Now it was Katrina's turn to look surprised. "Can't you see that? Wherever Cindy stepped, it's as if there is a path of golden flowers. I'm feeling better now. Let's go again. I'll lead, so I can follow the trail. Let's catch up with Cindy," she said, and the two girls started walking through the ferns on their way to find their friend.

Chapter 6

Moving toward the valley, Cindy entered another copse of trees. She was awestruck with the majesty towering above her. As she moved into the denseness of the forest once again, she was swallowed up by the beauty that surrounded her. There were many types of trees here. While some looked like redwoods, others appeared to be evergreens. Their colors were different from the ones she was used to seeing at home. Looking up at the trees, she imagined how fun it would be to be able to climb to the top of the tree canopy, picturing the breathtaking beauty that fascinated her. Pulling her thoughts back to the task at hand, she wondered what is in the valley? She moved forward while she continued to look at the trees. She noticed the pine needles were changing to the fall colors of deciduous trees in her world. The colors were vibrant as they descended on each tree. It was as if a can of paint had been poured over the tree with the brightest color appearing at the top and then losing its hue as it flowed to the bottom. The yellows were like the golden aspens in the Colorado mountains, and the reds were a deep red like the maples she had remembered when they visited Kansas, but the most magnificent needles were the ones that had the glow of orange, red and yellow all in the same tree.

Advancing toward the valley, she was struck with a great excruciating pain and agony like a knife penetrating through her mind. She grasped her head while her knees buckled underneath her. She couldn't move, and a scream caught in her throat. She felt as if she were struck by lightning. The focus of pain hit her on the forehead as she heard a piercing cry like a dentist drill on stone.

An eerie glow crept across the ground like a boa constrictor grabbing its victim poised to attack. Suddenly, she felt a tentacle grabbing at her, dragging her across the ground. As she was pulled across the rough ground, she felt her skin peel away like being pulled across the road. She moved her hand to grasp her charm and clung to it in a death grip as she felt the charm warming. The tentacle hissed like a fire as you poured water on it, and it melted away.

She tried to turn back and run into the woods but could not move. As she looked at the white group of animals she had felt pulled toward, she felt confused. They looked like a herd of white horses, but it was difficult for her to see them clearly. It was almost as if she was looking through an opaque piece of glass. It looked as if the glass covered the horses in a sort of dome. She felt that she was still being pulled toward the dome in the valley. Her only option was to move forward, closer to the scorched land. Her nose was assaulted by the odor of sulfur, like rotten eggs, surrounding her as she took her first steps.

Being drawn closer to the valley, she bumped into what felt like a smooth glass window. It sloped away from her as she reached up. She saw white forms cowering together. Her vision was blurring as the glass appeared to be frosted, but as she held tight to her charm, her vision cleared. She could see!

What she saw was a horrific view of white horses' foreheads bleeding and scabbing over, and the ground was speckled with blood. As the horses moved, Cindy could see the terror in their eyes. Her eyes widened as she saw their glowing white coats change. The fur on the horses was fading to a ghostly gray. Cindy had to turn away from the frightful sight.

When she turned, she heard a dreadful whinny, and she saw a horrendous looking creature with a glaring scar running down his back covered with scraggly raven colored hair. His pants were made of fur that shimmered in the light like moon beams. An acrid smell of rotting flesh wafted from him on the breeze as she tried to move toward the horses. Unable to move forward, she slid her hands along the glasslike surface and tried to find a way to enter the dome-like structure. At the same time, she saw a horse with a white coat turn gray as the evil creature continued the work of detaching a golden horn from the forehead of the frightened animal. Once removed, The Hunter pushed the horn through a link of a chain he wore around his neck. The links were nearly full with a variety of many-colored horns. When the final unicorn lost its horn, the force field creating the dome completely dissolved. The Hunter moved away from Cindy, across the destroyed valley with his necklace of unicorn horns hanging from his neck.

Cindy started to rush toward the wicked creature that had caused so much harm, but before she could get very far, a massive black unicorn stood in front of her, pushing her back into a stand of trees. It continued to push her back toward the copse of trees until she couldn't move forward at all. As the unicorn held her back at the edge of the valley, her friends came toward her. They gasped at the sight of the black unicorn standing over six feet tall in front of them. They trembled with fear as they looked up at the massive creature.

It looked at Cindy, and suddenly she could hear a voice in her head. It was the unicorn who was speaking to her.

"Do not be afraid. I am Lunar! I am the one who has called you here. My herd has been defeated by The Hunter. He has stolen our power for his plans to destroy our world. In this state of desperation, I summoned you here for the talents each of you have, to help me, as the last unicorn with power. I need you to restore the horns of the unicorns of my herd, the horns that have been stolen by The Hunter, just like those of so many before."

Cindy turned to Katrina and Gia. "Did you hear what Lunar said?"

Gia asked, "Who's Lunar?"

Cindy said, "This is Lunar." Then she repeated what she had just heard from the massive black unicorn.

"How can you know what he said?" Katrina asked quietly.

Cindy said, "I don't know. I can just hear him."

"We are just kids. We have no power! We are just ordinary kids," Gia said.

Lunar looked at Cindy again. "As we work together, you will realize the potential each of you has within."

Chapter 7

Lunar had tried to follow the girls' conversation and give them time to get used to the fact that they were in an unfamiliar land and an unfamiliar situation. Then he ran out of patience and interrupted their talking. He had to find a way without making them angry. He whinnied. All three girls turned towards him. It was as if a trance had been broken, and they remembered that he was there.

"How did you get away from the destruction of that hideous creature?" Cindy asked.

"I have been shunned by my herd because of my black coloring. They have been afraid of me because I am different, and they wanted to blame me for their ill fate. I am no different than they are, although it seems I am the only one able to summon help from another world. When I felt the evil coming, they did not believe me, and by the time they caught his scent, it was too late. He had already started a fire to burn us out of our hiding place. The other unicorns were easily seen because of their glowing white fur. I, with black fur, was able to hide in the shadows."

"That's totally not right! Just because of your color, you were teased and not believed," Katrina said after Cindy shared what Lunar had said.

"I am really surprised that they couldn't smell that creature. I could smell him as soon as I came upon the black scorched valley. He smells of rot and death," Cindy said, heading down to the dark circle.

"We must hurry. We don't have a lot of time. Once unicorns lose our horns, they have ten days before they will end up being horses forever. I believe it is safe to go back down to the herd. The Hunter is gone," Lunar told Cindy.

The girls and Lunar approached the herd. The unicorns were gray; their luminescence was fading even more as their hair turned to the dusky color.

The smell of soot and burnt land terrified Cindy. She remembered the odor of her house and the forest burning. She saw the flash of flames and the animals that were burnt as her family escaped the fire. She had to get that thought out of her mind. She had to focus on the unicorns here; she saw the red spots from where they were burnt. What was so very hard for her was to look into their fear-filled eyes as they spoke to Lunar. The girls stood silently while the herd seemed to speak to each other.

"Why have you brought the humans here? Hasn't their race destroyed us enough?"

"I summoned them from another world. They are pure and innocent. I know they can help us."

"But you brought The Hunter upon us to destroy us."

"I did not! I had nothing to do with him finding us. I am not evil. I have a power unknown to you. Remember, I am the one who told you to move. I felt The Hunter approaching long before any of you realized we were in danger. You didn't listen to me. If you had, we may not have become overtaken."

"Enough, all of you!" A heavily pregnant mare moved forward. "I know you let fear blind you from clear thinking. We have about ten days before we will be forever horses." Then she turned to Gia.

Gia sensed by the body language of the pregnant unicorn that she wanted Gia to move nearer. When she touched the mare, she heard a voice in her head saying, "I am called Moonbeam. Come here, Pure Ones."

Turning to Katrina and Cindy, Gia said, "Moonbeam would like you to come toward her. She has called us Pure Ones."

As the girls approached, Gia felt a tingling sensation. She touched Moonbeam's belly and knew that there was a power within Moonbeam's womb. She felt a kick against her hand and smiled. She sensed an urgency to help her give birth. She remembered the many times when she was visiting her aunt over the summer and how she had learned to help when mares were giving birth.

Gia spoke quietly to Moonbeam. "Your foal is ready to come."

"Yes, my little ones are coming."

Chapter 8

"We need to move away from this dreadful place. Lunar can you show us where a safe place is where we will be able to hide from The Hunter, so he will not be able to see you," Cindy said.

The unicorns reluctantly looked at Lunar and started to complain about the pain and the hurt they had already experienced. One told that they were already exhausted from the whole ordeal with The Hunter burning them out of their valley and surrounding them with roaring flames of fire.

A young unicorn whose coat is quickly turning a dusky gray whined, "Haven't we had enough today? The Hunter used his power to subdue us and then proceeded to torture us and wrangle off our horns? Isn't that enough?"

Moonbeam looked at the unicorn who was complaining. "Starscape, stop! My young ones cannot be born in the open. We all need to be hidden to be protected. You need to be protected! The elders need to be protected! Lunar knows of a safe place. We need to follow him." Starscape turned away and moved back through the herd. Gia moved toward Moonbeam and spoke with her. "I can find some plants to help ease the pain of your herd and soothe their burns after we move further into the forest for protection." Mind speaking, Moonbeam said, "Yes, that would be wonderful." She then shared the information with the herd.

Moonbeam headed toward the herd encouraging them to move from the black barren ground and head in the direction Lunar was leading them. All the unicorns followed Lunar along an overgrown path full of underbrush, some stumbling along the way. Finally, they arrived at a large tree in the forest. Lunar placed his horn to the tree which opened up to a tunnel. They passed through the tunnel into a small valley with luscious green grass and an array of rainbow flowers. The tree tunnel closed after them, so they were protected and could take some time to recover.

Cindy and Katrina, "Come over, so we can look for some plants to soothe the burns of the unicorns and I might be able to find some other plants to help them relax."

"How do you know there will be the same kinds of plants in this world as at our home?" Cindy asked.

"I don't, but I am hoping to find some, but I do know that there are many plants around our world that have been used to heal and soothe burns."

"Have you thought to ask Moonbeam if she knows any plants that will help the unicorns?" Katrina asked.

"No, I haven't, but she really needs to rest. Can't you see she is exhausted and add to that she will give birth anytime now to her baby," Gia said.

"I could ask Lunar," Cindy suggested as Gia looked around the area.

"No need to ask. I already see many plants I could use. There are several blackberry bushes. I also see sumac, rosemary, lavender, red clover, greenbriar and prickly pear."

"What! You mean the plants you mentioned can help the unicorns? I never knew there were so many plants that have healing properties?" Katrina said, astonished.

"I am hungry. I would like to eat some of those luscious blackberries," Cindy said.

"Yes, I think we all could use a little something to eat before we gather plants. Did you know that some of the plants I mentioned were used for medicine by the Native Americans as well as for food?"

"No way, how do you know that? I'm not about to eat raw wild plants other than black berries. I know they are good," Katrina said.

"How fascinating! I'd love to try some different plants to eat," Cindy said.

As the girls headed over to the blackberry bushes, they noticed that some of the unicorns were nibbling on some red clover and the spring green grasses around them. They also noticed many of the unicorns dropped down to the ground as soon as they arrived in the meadow.

Gia stopped in her tracks. "We need to find some water for the unicorns. They have just collapsed on the ground from dehydration."

"The blackberries are going to be very juicy. I would think it would help to bring some to the dehydrated ones," Cindy said.

"Yes, hurry and gather some, Cindy."

"Katrina, come help us,"

"No way! I'm starving, I am going to eat some of these blackberries first," Katrina said as the berry juice dripped from her mouth.

Cindy thought to herself, *"What a selfish brat."*

Chapter 9

Gia and Cindy gathered as many of the berries as they could, but it was only enough to bring a handful at a time to the unicorns that had fallen to the ground.

"Is there any way we could get more berries to these exhausted elders? "Cindy said.

Gia thought for a moment, "We could cut the branches off with my Swiss Army pocket knife. It has a scissor tool on it. We could cut the branches with several berries on them."

"Why don't you cut the branches, and then I will bring them to the unicorns?"

Katrina, come over here and help.

"You have had plenty of time to eat berries. It is time for you to stop thinking of yourself and help the unicorns!" Gia shouted.

"What am I supposed to do? It looks like you and Cindy have taken care of several of the unicorns already?"

"You can go over to that large patch of lavender and pick the leaves and the purple flowers and put them in a pile next to you. I will use the lavender to relax the rest of the herd. There is also rosemary near the lavender. Pick off the leaves of the rosemary that are more of a bright green and the blue flowers are growing lengthwise instead of on the end of the stems. They are long and thin like evergreen needles. I will use the rosemary to help relieve the muscle pain of the unicorns."

Katrina yelled back at Gia, "I know what lavender looks like because Mom has it in the house, but I've never seen a rosemary bush."

Gia stopped what she was doing and turned toward Katrina. "It smells like spaghetti sauce, and it's right beside the lavender. Try looking for it." Then she turned back to the unicorns.

Reluctantly Katrina headed to the area that Gia had pointed out. "It smells like spaghetti sauce, and it's right next to the lavender," she said snidely under her breath. Then she stopped and said to herself, "So that's what rosemary looks like," and started to pick off the leaves and flowers as the other girls finished with the dehydrated unicorns.

Gia and Cindy looked around the herd and saw that most of the unicorns were now resting. They headed over to the blackberry bushes hoping to find some blackberries for themselves, but there were not many left.

Being extremely hungry and tired, Cindy looked at Gia and asked, "Are there any other plants nearby that we could eat?"

Just as Gia was about to answer, Lunar came over and spoke to Cindy, "Thank you so much for helping the herd settle and relax. Get on my back and I will take you down to the water edge. You can have a drink and you can eat the cattails to give you more strength."

"You mean you can eat cattails and you won't get sick," Cindy mindspoke with Lunar.

"Yes, they are one of the best survival plants around. You can find them anywhere around the world where there's water."

Cindy turned to Gia and said, "Did you know that we can eat cattail plants?"

"Yes, the indigenous population used it for food. It is one of the most popular survival foods. People have been eating it for centuries. How did you know that?"

"Lunar was saying thank you for helping the herd, and he wants us to ride on his back down to the pond to get some water and to eat some cattails."

Arriving at the pond, the girls got off Lunar's back and walked to the edge of the pond. Kneeling to drink, they noticed how clear the water was. They could see all the way to the bottom of the pond. As they took their first drink, they had not realized how thirsty they were. They gulped down the water to soothe their dry throats. Curiously looking at the cattails, they were stumped on how to eat them. Lunar showed them to just bite them. Being quite hungry, they gingerly took a nibble, not liking the bitter taste of the outer layer and spit it out immediately.

Lunar laughed as he looked at Cindy. Mindspeaking, he said, "Peel the outer layer off. Then bite the inside."

At first the taste was bitter, but as Cindy continued to nibble at the inside of the plant, she was surprised that it started to taste sweet like sugar cane.

Smiling, she told Gia, "Peel off the brown fuzzy part and bite into the green flesh of the plant. You are in for a big surprise!"

As Gia bit into the crunchy green flesh, she was amazed at the sweet taste that flooded into her mouth.

"Wow, this is so good, and with the juice, I bet it would serve as a nice refreshing drink. Let's pick some more and bring it back with us and let Katrina try it.

When Gia and Cindy arrived back with the herd, Katrina came over and said, "Here are the two piles of plants. What shall we do now?"

"Sleep. We're exhausted," Gia said.

"We have been on the go all day," Cindy said.

"What are you doing with those cattail plants?" Katrina asked.

"It's our dinner!" Cindy said. "Just bite into it. The outside is a little tough, but the inside is worth it."

"You've got to be kidding! No thanks, I am still full of all the blackberries I ate."

Gia turned to Cindy. Taking a cattail from her hand, Gia cut it lengthwise and cut a slice off it and handed it to Katrina.

"Just try, it is like eating sugar cane; it is sweet and juicy. It's not bad at all."

"Ok I will try it." After skeptically taking a bite, she smiled and said, "Wow, that is good, but I still like the blackberries better. I truly am still full of the blackberries. Besides my stomach sort of hurts." Katrina said.

Gia walked away from the girls and went over to where Moonbeam was resting. As she made her way to Moonbeam, she kept her distance from the other unicorns but was also evaluating how the herd looked. Most of them were peacefully sleeping.

Moonbeam lifted her head, mindspeaking to Gia. "Thanks so much for your help; if you would like to sleep near me, I would like that, but I will understand if you want to sleep with your friends."

"I need to sleep with Cindy and Katrina, especially Katrina. She has never slept in the open and is quite uncomfortable about sleeping on the hard ground."

"If you lie down in the ferns, you will find that they are soft like cotton, and they will help keep you warmer than on the open ground," Moonbeam said.

"Thanks, I will let them know."

Once she crossed back to where Cindy and Katrina were, they were both sound asleep. Gia settled down in a fern near the other girls. Overcome by the beauty of the sky full of beautiful stars, she gazed up at them and quickly fell asleep.

Gia startled awake but couldn't figure out what had caused her to awaken.

Chapter 10

"Gia! Help! Wake up! The time has come!" Moonbeam was crying out.

Gia shook her head, not quite sure where the cry came from, foggy from being awakened out of a deep sleep. She thought, *"Time for what?"*

Hearing a ear piercing whinney, she ran over to Moonbeam, tripping over Katrina and Cindy in her rush, waking them as another whinny of agony penetrated the air. She rushed forward, finally arriving near Moonbeam who was covered with sweat and breathing hard.

"Katrina, get the lavender you picked yesterday and bring it over here fast. I need to use it to calm Moonbeam as she continues to give birth," Gia said.

Lunar galloped over to where his mate was, concern for her clear in his eyes. It was a rare occurrence when a unicorn was born.

Cindy went over to be close to Lunar to comfort him, and she petted his temples to help him become calm and understand that everything would be ok.

Even though Gia didn't completely understand Moonbeam's language, she knew the language of birth. With a loud whinny and a bursting of water, Moonbeam's breathing quickened as she pushed out the foal. First one came. It wasn't breathing. The mucus around its nose needed to be wiped away. Gia called Cindy and Katrina, "Come help me."

Katrina took one look and said, "No way! I can't." She turned pale and sat down, looking away and afraid she was going to be sick.

Cindy rushed forward. "What do I do? How can I help?"

"Start by pulling the mucus away from the nose. The first priority is to help the foal breathe."

Cindy quickly moved forward to help clear away the mucus from the foal's nose and eyes as the foal coughed and snorted, making wheezing sounds as if it was difficult for him to breathe. He passed out.

In desperation, Cindy pulled off her necklace and placed it on his chest. When she touched his chest, she felt a fiery sensation, and her hands felt like they were burning. Then a feeling of cold filled her body as if she had an icy hot cream that could be rubbed on the muscles that were having a hard time breathing. In a panic, she continued to hug and move the charm on the totally black foal.

Overcome by a calm soothing peace, she heard a whisper on the wind bringing the breath of spring scents of lilac and orange blossoms flooding her nose. A feeling of life flowed over her like a feather being brushed over her fingertips as the foal took his first breath. The cold within her waned as if the sun came out from behind a cloud.

"I am alive. Do not be afraid. You have saved my life. I am Obsidian. We are connected. You must be my guardian, and I will be yours as we journey together to unite our herd and defeat The Hunter."

Cindy felt rather than heard the message coming from the foal and stared at the tiny unicorn in silence.

"Oh no. There is another one coming out now." Gia continued to soothe and calm Moonbeam as the horse gave birth once again.

Lunar came forward to help clean off the second foal. This one was white as cotton, and her horn was a twist of silver and gold intertwined. The other unicorns of the herd huddled together, terrified of these unusual foals.

Katrina turned around and was amazed by the beauty of the two foals. When the light reflected on the female's horn, it shone with hues of purple and pink and reflected off her twin's golden horn. "Wow, they are gorgeous. I love the one with the silver and gold twisted horn, and I love the encirclement of the reflected hues of purple and pink."

"What do you mean? I only see the shimmering white coat and the silver and gold twisted horn," Gia said.

Katrina was entranced by the white foal. As she reached out her hand to stroke the foal's nose, a sizzling sensation ran through her fingers and up her arms until she was encircled by the purple glow and felt a connection like none she had ever felt before.

In her mind, she heard the words, "I am Amethyst."

Startled, Katrina removed her hand from the foal's nose. As she did this, she felt a slight chill, and she looked back into the foal's eyes. She was drawn again to pet the foal.

"I have chosen you to be my guardian. You will need to protect me from the evil magic that The Hunter has cast upon us with the light that has been given to you and the sight to see paths to safety."

"Okay, Amethyst," Katrina said aloud.

Gia rubbed Moonbeam down as she continued to complete the birthing process. "Who are you talking to?" Gia asked.

"Umm, this is Amethyst. She has chosen me as her guardian to protect her from The Hunter," Katrina said.

"I delivered the foal, and she chose YOU to be her guardian? You wouldn't even look at the birth. How do you know she has chosen you?"

"She told me so right after she was born. You saw when I petted her nose, I heard her in my head."

Gia was shocked. How had Katrina heard from the foal when she hadn't?

"How in the world are you going to be her guardian? You rarely think of anyone but yourself," Gia said.

"What do you mean I only care about myself?" Katrina said.

"During the whole time we have been here, you have been selfish in only wanting to be comfortable and to go back home," Gia said.

"I have changed. I have a new purpose and light to protect Amethyst. She has spoken to me," Katrina said, as the young foal leaned against her.

"I don't believe you. I bet you will continue to think only of yourself when danger comes," Cindy said.

"Stop!" Lunar whinnied. "We need to work together and set aside our differences. We only have eight days before all of the herd will become horses forever."

Gia and Katrina jumped as they saw Lunar's eye start to blaze red as he whinnied loudly.

"Cindy move! Lunar has gone mad!"

"No, he hasn't. He is upset that you and Katrina are raising your voices at each other."

Moonbeam added, "We are stronger together than apart."

"I'm sorry Moonbeam, you are right. We are stronger together than apart," Gia said as she looked at the ground, ashamed of her outburst at Katrina.

"It has been difficult for us to accept differences. Our fear of those different from us coming from within the herd has weakened our power, not because of Lunar's color but because of the group's shunning him. You thought he was evil," she said, turning to the herd. "The only evil here is The Hunter because of our broken unity."

"Is there even a way to restore our power?" shouted Starscape.

"Yes, there is a way, but in order for it to be effective, we need to be united again. I have brought these friends here to help us," said Lunar pointing his horn toward the three girls."

"The night is coming. Where are we going to sleep?" said Katrina with a yawn.

"We will be sleeping on the ground with the unicorns. It's wonderful to look up at the open sky. It will be a stunning sight to see all the stars," Gia said.

"But the ground is so hard, and there will be no light. How will I see?" said Katrina. "You don't need light to sleep. Besides, the moon may shine like the sun if it is full tonight," said Cindy.

Katrina felt exposed again. She curled up close to Amethyst. Being close to the foal gave her comfort. She felt the foal's warmth and was content. Then the adult unicorns encircled the girls and the foals. The night was dark and scary for Katrina who woke up to every sound she heard. She was terrified at the crunching of leaves, afraid that some terrible creature was approaching. When she started to scream out, she saw that it was Lunar coming back from a walk.

Snuggling closer to Amethyst, she continued to be warmed by the foal's soft fur and as she listened to her breathing, she began to feel more peaceful and less frightened. A gentle light breeze skimmed across Katrina's face, and Amethyst's mane tickled her nose.

Chapter 11

Awakening before everyone else, Gia headed over to where the two piles of lavender and rosemary were placed. Using a large piece of bark that had a bowl-like indentation in it and some rocks, she started blending the two plants together and adding some water to make a salve. She carried the batch over to where the unicorns with the worst burns were, but as soon as she approached them, they bolted away from her.

"I just want to help cover your burns so they won't get infected," Gia said aloud, knowing that they couldn't understand her.

Moonbeam awakened, overwhelmed with the frustration and sadness of the emotions Gia was feeling. She trotted over to where Gia was and nuzzled her to let her know she would be able to help.

"I just want to help cover your burns so they won't get infected," Gia said aloud, knowing that they couldn't understand her.

Moonbeam awakened, overwhelmed with the frustration and sadness of the emotions Gia was feeling. She trotted over to where Gia was and nuzzled her to let her know she would be able to help.

"Gia, I know the herd is still uncomfortable with you helping them. I will walk with you over to where the unicorns are and explain to them that the poultice will help heal their burns."

"Why are they so skittish? They know I helped you give birth to your foals. Isn't that enough for them to know I am here to help?"

"They saw that you helped me, but with the strangeness of the powers displayed by the foals, and their connections with your friends, they are even more frightened thinking that you will use the power to harm instead of help them."

"Why would they think we wanted to hurt them? We are stuck in this world, sort of against our own wills also."

Unicorns in general are leery of humans approaching them, especially with how easily it seemed for The Hunter to overtake us. In past history, humans have been extremely deceiving and initially taken advantage of our trust. Too many have forced fair maidens to coax the unicorn out of hiding to come near, and before they knew what happened, a net was flung over them, and they were caught. Many were killed."

"How cruel and evil humans seem to have been in this land. How did they come to be so evil?"

"That my dear will be a story for later. We need to get the herd healthy, and moving by this afternoon. Lunar wishes to discuss why and how we are heading to a magical valley that's a few days' journey away from here in order to make a potion to help restore our horns and the magic that comes with regeneration of the horns."

"That would mean when we arrive at the magical valley, the unicorns would have only about five days before they would be forever horses."

Both Cindy and Katrina awoke to the rustling of baby unicorns next to their bodies. They smiled at each other over the heads of their young charges and reached out to pet the foals. Both Obsidian and Amethyst opened their eyes and looked around for their mother. Without any words for their guardians, they stood and started running through the forest.

"Wait," yelled Katrina, taking her role of guardian seriously.

Amethyst turned toward her and sent her a message. "We're going to help our mother."

Katrina yelled again. "We'll come to help, too."

Cindy was following right behind. "Help who? Only being able to hear one unicorn at a time is frustrating."

Katrina responded. "They're going to find Moonbeam."

Cindy said, "That makes sense. We must still be half asleep. Don't lose sight of them."

"I can see the path they're leaving across the camp."

Unicorns cleared a path for the oncoming unicorn foals and the two unwelcome human girls.

"I wish they wouldn't do that," said Cindy. "We're not going to hurt them."

"They don't know that yet," said Katrina. "We'll have to find a way to let them know that we're safe."

The sun was just peeking through the branches of the trees when the foals found their mother, and the three girls were reunited.

"Wow, those little ones can really run!" Gia said with some surprise in her voice.

"They led us straight to you and Moonbeam. How are things going with treating the burns?" asked Cindy.

"Not well," said Gia with a frown. "They don't trust me. Moonbeam is talking with them now." She turned toward the herd and saw Moonbeam leading an elder mare with burns on her flank.

Moonbeam spoke through her mind to Gia. "She's hesitant, but the pain is too much for her, and she wants to try your medicine. I told her you were gentle and kind and knew many recipes to help us with our wounds."

Gia swallowed hard. She thanked Moonbeam and hoped she wouldn't disappoint her.

Gently, she approached the mare and let her smell her hand. Then she reached between her ears to give her a gentle scratch. When the mare didn't bolt, she asked Moonbeam to tell her that she was going to apply the poultice and to explain that it only had herbs that she would eat herself. Then she laughed and said that she probably wouldn't eat them together though.

Gia gently applied the healing mixture to the burns and other than the flank quivering, the mare didn't move. When she was done, she returned to the mare's head.

Moonbeam passed on a message from the mare. "She says to tell you that you are indeed a gifted healer and that she will gladly tell the others that they should come to see you for their care."

Cindy suddenly heard Lunar's voice in her head. "Please come see me. Please leave Obsidian with Moonbeam; he will be safe. I have something vitally important to discuss with you."

Cindy swallowed hard and mindspoke back. "Where are you?"

Again Lunar's voice was in her head. "Just tell Gia and Katrina that you'll be right back and then start walking back the way you came. I will find you."

Cindy did just that and started walking back into the forest while the remaining unicorns in the herd started lining up to receive Gia's treatment. She was smiling and very happy. Katrina did not look very happy. It was her job to keep track of two rambunctious foals away from a line of grumpy elderly unicorns.

Approaching Lunar, Cindy greeted him with a tight hug around his neck.

"I have missed you. It was quite an episode helping Obsidian being born and then not being able to move very far away from him without him being at my heels. I am glad to have a little break. What is it that you need to talk to me about?"

"We need to make a three day journey to a magical valley in order to make a potion that will regenerate the horns of my herd. I need your help in making the potion because I have no hands to mix and stir the formula."

"How do you know of this valley?"

"When my mother and I were banished from our herd by my father because of my coat color, we found a secure place to stay that ended up having magical plants that allowed us to grow stronger and more magical than the rest of our herd. One of the most powerful plants was the Everberry bush. On occasion, we saw animals that had been injured eat those berries and they were able to regrow limbs that were destroyed."

"You mean by eating these berries they were able to regenerate damaged limbs like some lizards in our world would grow back a tail after it was broken off? So why did you have to talk to me about this? What am I to do with this information?"

"I want you to share this information with your friends so they can understand why we need to leave our camp and to know why it is vital that we head on this journey. Otherwise the unicorns will be gone forever."

"Do any of the other unicorns know of this valley?"

"Yes. Moonbeam does. She would visit me often after we were banished by my father from the safety and security of our herd."

"You mean your own father didn't want you or your mother? What a terrible father he must have been?"

As Lunar and Cindy walked back toward the herd, Cindy said, "I feel like my father doesn't really want me because I am a girl, but I am grateful that he loves my mom."

Lunar was pleased to see that the unicorns had finally started to trust the girls and the atmosphere of the camp was one of peace. All the unicorns had their wounds covered in the mixture that Gia had made for them. They were around the girls enjoying the attention that was given to them.

Once Obsidian spied Cindy, he darted away from Katrina's grasp. He tore toward Cindy, nuzzling her with his nose in his excitement. He pushed Cindy into Lunar's side.

"Slow down there, kiddo," Lunar said.

Looking at the ground, Obsidian said, "I'm sorry, Dad. I didn't know my own strength. I felt very uncomfortable and fearful when I was away from my guardian."

"I am glad that your bond is so strong with Cindy. You will have to work together in the future to protect each other." Then Lunar turned to the group of unicorns in front of him. "Attention all unicorns. Gather round. We need to plan on moving forward to a new camp."

"Why do we need to move to a new camp? We have shelter, water, and food. We have all we need to stay safe and hidden," a grumpy elder spoke up. "We are still needing to rest and recover from the attack, and Moonbeam just gave birth to twins. Don't you think she needs to rest more?"

Moonbeam rose to stand with Lunar. Her foals and the girls followed.

Moonbeam spoke. "Have you forgotten that we have only eight days before our kind will vanish forever and we will just be a shell of horses with no magic or power? Is that how you want to live out your lives?"

"It doesn't seem like a bad thing to me. I've lived a good life."

Lunar said, "I will not force you to follow. The choice will be yours to make, but hear me out before you pass judgment on me. I know of a magical valley a three day journey from here. I stayed in the valley with my mother, Star, after my father, Knight, sent us away. The more time I spent in this place, the stronger I became. I have witnessed a plant called the Everberry that heals. I am sure that by eating this plant in some form, our horns will be restored, and we can overtake The Hunter once and for all."

"That's impossible! Why should we believe or trust you especially since you have brought more humans into our land?" a light gray stallion spoke up.

"Starscape, I know that you're my twin brother, and if you choose to stay in the horse state forever, that's fine with me, that will be your choice not mine," Lunar said, narrowing his eyes at his twin. "However, all the unicorns need to be given the opportunity to make their own choice."

Katrina looked toward the horizon and saw a sun soaked trail with a purplish pink light calling to her. Moving toward the path, she noticed yellow flowers shimmering in the light. She leaned toward Cindy and Gia and spoke quietly.

"Look at that trail of light emerging through the grass over there," Katrina said.

"I don't see any lighted path anywhere. I just see miles and miles of grass ocean," said Gia.

"I don't see any lighted path either. I only see buttercup flowers. I don't remember seeing them yesterday," said Cindy.

Amethyst trotted over to where Katrina was looking and moved closer to the path of buttercup flowers with the purple-pink reflection. She placed her horn to the ground and suddenly everyone could see the path.

The other unicorns noticed where the girls were looking and turned their heads looking in the same direction as Katrina, now alert and looking around. They hadn't noticed anything new. They only saw the barren valley, black, like death.

Gia turned to Cindy and said, "How could Katrina see that? I couldn't, could you?" Cindy shook her head. "Remember what Lunar said. We all have special gifts. Hers must have something to do with purple and pink trails."

Lunar said, "Wow! This path is close to the way I was going to be leading the herd to the magical valley where we will find the Everberry bush and the other ingredients we need to restore our horns' magic. Let's move. We need to be on our way."

Starscape, being the younger brother of Lunar, always had a negative attitude toward anything Lunar said or did. "How do we know it's safe? How do we know it's not a trick to lure us into the hands of the enemy?" he protested.

"Would you rather go toward the dark, or would you rather go toward the light?" Moonbeam said.

"I still don't trust these beings. How do we know they are good?" Starscape said.

"They helped me save my foals. If they were evil, they wouldn't have helped me or connected to my babies," Moonbeam said.

"It is time to decide if you will trust and follow me and these girls or live the rest of your lives as an empty shell of a horse with no magic and die alone," Lunar spoke.

"That's a bit harsh don't you think, Lunar?" Cindy mind spoke.

"It's the hard truth. They need to understand what they are saying yes to if they choose to stay here."

Chapter 12

Katrina and Amethyst were at the head of the parade of unicorns traveling to a new camp. Lunar was bringing up the rear and keeping watch over the herd. The path through the field was steady, but it also left the unicorns exposed as they crossed the open space. As they traveled, they saw many flying creatures they hadn't seen before. They hoped the creatures wouldn't attack from the sky. They didn't know whether these silvery scaled creatures were friends or foes and with wingspans spreading five feet wide, the herd became nervous. The creatures reminded the girls of the pterodactyls they had seen pictures of in books when they were studying prehistory.

Lunar, feeling the restlessness of the herd, quickly joined Obsidian and Amethyst. Together, they created a shield of protection around the herd. Only then did they continue on their way. It was not a minute too soon. The creatures of the sky tried to attack them. With a loud clanging of talons on the strong transparent shield, the creatures tried to harm the unicorns. With the loud clashing of talons on glass, the unicorns bucked and reared in a panic. They peered upward searching to see if there were cracks appearing in the shield. Some unicorns bucked and reared in their panic. They wanted to get away, but there was nowhere to go. Several became disoriented and wanted to run straight for the protection of the woods they had left. Others ran in the opposite direction. Terrified and confused, the thundering herd kept running into the sides of the shield and getting knocked in the head, intensifying the pain they had already received from the loss of their horns.

Amethyst mindspoke, "Katrina, I need you to come close to me. We need to calm the herd before they destroy the shield. Place your right hand on my horn and hold up your left hand. Close your eyes and picture a burst of sunlight to cover the entire interior of the shield. As you picture the sunshine, once you feel a warming sensation, you can open your eyes. I will be sending out a calming scent, and together we will quiet the herd."

Katrina pictured the sunlight as Amethyst had instructed her. As she visualized the brilliance, she pictured the radiance of sunbeams. She also found herself visualizing rose petals falling like snow around the herd as if to hide them from the eyes of the flying creatures. She felt silken petals brush against her skin while she felt the warming sensation all through her body. She opened her eyes, surprised to see the shield filled with sunlight and rose petals dropping from the sky onto the ground and on the unicorns within the shield.

Cindy and Gia looked at each other, too shocked to speak.

Finally, Gia said, "Did you know Katrina could do that?"

Cindy shook her head in silence. "Did you?"

Gia responded in the same manner. "Not a clue."

They looked back at Katrina. Next, Amethyst opened her mouth and let out a calming scent of lavender and jasmine scented air. The unicorns were overcome with a sense of serenity, and as they reacted to the calming sensation, they became less skittish. Soon, they were tranquil enough to listen when Lunar spoke.

"Stay together. Trust me, even if the clanging starts again. You are safe and secure. Let us gallop the last few hundred yards toward the protection of trees and regroup once we get to cover."

"Wait! We can't run as fast as horses, we need to be able to keep up. How will that work if you all go cantering towards the protection of the woods?"

Lunar looked at Cindy and said, "Hop on the backs of Obsidian, Amethyst and Moonbeam. You all have ridden horses, right?"

Cindy said, "Wait, let me check." She passed the message on to Gia and Katrina.

"It will be so much fun to ride on the backs of unicorns, but we don't have a saddle," Katrina said hesitantly.

"I am not sure how to ride a unicorn either," Cindy said.

"The herd is starting to get restless again. Hurry up and get on your unicorns," Lunar mindspoke.

"How do I get on the unicorn?" Cindy cried out.

Gia climbed off Moonbeam and helped Cindy get onto Obsidian who was also nervous about having someone on his back.

Amethyst told Katrina to hurry up. "I need you to help me calm the herd again. I'll lie down and just get onto me; please hurry."

Just as Katrina climbed onto Amethyst, a scraping sound was heard above them. They looked up to see a bird stretch out its wings so that it blocked the sunlight from the outside of the protective dome. Soon, it began pecking the top of the shield. A sound like a baseball bat hitting the side of an oil drum reverberated throughout. Suddenly, there was a crack as the beak poked through the shield. Another bird slid onto the top of the dome, and the first slid sideways raking its eight inch talons down the side of the dome. A break started to form from the top to the side. It sounded like the earth splitting apart.

Obsidian and Lunar saw another huge creature hit, and a talon came in toward the last few unicorns from the herd. They saw it rake across Starscape, and they both turned and pointed their horns at the talon. Its owner let out a high pitched screech that shattered the shield.

Amethyst created a purple smoke screen that allowed the rest of the creatures to scatter, and the herd ran straight for the forest a few yards away.

Chapter 13

Now, they were hidden in a strange type of rainforest with dense plants and ferns covering both sides of the path. The ferns were as tall as apple trees and formed an arc of visual protection for them as the first day of travel ended. They prepared camp under the dense forest of trees and ferns. As the girls settled down, the earth felt like a feather bed, and they were sure they could sleep comfortably.

"Cindy, could you ask Katrina if she knows how much further the path is to the valley?" Lunar asked.

"Katrina, Lunar wants to know if you know how far it is to the valley?"

"This is really irritating. I wish we all could hear each other speak, so we wouldn't have to interpret each word and explain what is being said or asked of others."

"Yes, I know, but it's going to be like this all through our journey," said Cindy.

"No, I am not really sure, but I think it may be a day or two away. I can only see the path before me. I can't see where it ends."

"The elder unicorns are having a hard time moving so quickly. They are starting to become lame. I need to find cat's claw, aloe vera, white willow bark or lavender to help ease the pain of the older ones," said Gia.

"What did Gia just say?" Lunar asked.

"She was saying that the elder unicorns are becoming lame, and if we can't help them, they may not make it to the valley, and she wants to find some plants to help them," Cindy said in a rush.

"Yes, I am concerned for the elders also. I had noticed they were starting to misstep more than normal. What kind of plants? Lunar asked.

"Plants that will help the elders, so they are not in so much pain," Cindy said to Lunar.

"What do these plants look like? I'd like to help find them," said Katrina.

"I can help, also," said Cindy.

"Stay close. I don't want you wandering too far from the herd," Lunar said.

"Lunar wants us to stay close to the herd and not wander off too far away," Cindy said.

"Gessh, I feel like a little kid. Doesn't Lunar realize we have common sense, and we wouldn't go very far," Katrina complained.

Gia stopped the conversation and moved it on into the plan to find the herb.

"Cindy, can you look for cat's claw? It's a woody vine that has yellow flowers that spread out like a cat's claw and looks like hooked horns woven together," Gia said.

"Okay, but won't I need something to cut the vines with?"

"Yes. I forgot you don't have a pocket knife with you," Gia said.

"Obsidian, do you have a way to cut plants?" Cindy asked.

"My horn should be able to cut through a vine," Obsidian said.

Cindy turned to Gia. "We've got this covered."

"Katrina, can you look for Feverfew? It's a small bush that grows about twenty inches high. The flowers look like tiny daisies with bright yellow centers and have a citrus scent to them."

"Sounds good. Amethyst, will you come with me? To keep everyone happy, I don't want to wander out into the forest by myself," Katrina asked, turning toward the young unicorn.

"Sure, if it is okay with Lunar."

"If what is okay? What are you wanting to do?" Lunar asked.

"Geesh Dad, didn't you understand? Katrina wants to help gather plants, and she wants my company," Amethyst said.

Looking sternly at his daughter, "Watch your snippiness. I can only understand what Cindy is saying. I cannot understand Katrina or Gia."

Looking ashamed, Amethyst said, "I am sorry, Dad. I thought you could understand all of them."

"Well, I can't. Keep that in mind as we travel. Yes, you may go with Katrina to find the plants to help the elders," said Lunar.

"I will head over this direction. It looks like there is a willow tree. The leaves are serrated with a silvery white downy underside. Keep an eye out for each others' plants. We have a lot of hurting unicorns," said Gia.

Once everyone knew what they were to be looking for, each group headed out to start looking for the herbs that would provide relief for the elders who were on the verge of becoming lame.

As the girls began their search, the hornless unicorns settled down to graze on the sweet plants that tasted like citrus and honey. They were milling around when an enormous shadow approached them at high speed, bringing with it a splintering of branches, and creating a tornado of leaves which showered down on the unicorns. They quickly moved into protection formation with the stronger unicorns outside the circle, and the weaker ones inside the circle.

Barely missing the unicorns, a giant dragon landed on the ground with a belly flop causing the earth to shake. The wind was knocked out of the dragon's lungs and expelled with a burst of flame. It temporarily struggled to breathe from the impact on the landing.

Gia and the girls came running back to the herd, hoping the unicorns were safe. As they approached from different directions, they were all shocked to see a beautiful blue and golden dragon had crash landed near the herd.

Amethyst and Katrina arrived first to see what the commotion was. Then they ran quickly behind Moonbeam, scared by the gigantic creature that just landed next to the herd.

"Is he alive? I haven't seen a dragon since I was a young filly. I thought they were extinct," said Moonbeam quietly.

"Are dragons friendly, or are they like those other flying creatures that attacked us?" Amethyst whispered to her mother.

"Yes, most dragons are friendly. We used to travel together. We allowed the dragons to fly above us, so they could make sure it was safe for us to travel, and in return for their protection, we gave them the power to be camouflaged, so the dragon hunters couldn't see them."

"Katrina, let's go see the dragon," Amethyst said.

"No way! That thing could eat us alive, or kill us with just one breath!"

"My mom said that dragons are friendly. Besides, he hasn't moved yet. Trust me."

"I'm still not sure," Katrina said in a shaky voice.

"Don't be a coward. Remember, I will keep you safe. Besides, we need to trust each other to bond tightly."

Walking quietly over to where the dragon was, Amethyst and Katrina approached the creature. Just as Katrina bent down to get a closer look, the dragon's eyes fluttered open. Katrina screamed, Amethyst jumped at the scream, and the dragon rose to his feet ready to attack.

Lunar bounded over in a flash and stood between the dragon and Amethyst, staring as if speaking to the powerful creature.

Gia and Cindy came closer to the dragon, stunned at seeing the mythical beast.

Gia exclaimed, "How cool! A real live dragon! I have always been fascinated by books I've read about dragons, but seeing one in real-life is amazing!"

"Wow! What a beautiful creature," Cindy said.

Katrina told her friends, "Amethyst told me that Moonbeam told her that unicorns and dragons are friends and that the dragons used to lead the unicorns as they traveled around the world. We should be totally safe with this one."

Cindy leaned forward to touch the scales.

The dragon roared and tried to get away. Cindy jumped back with a glare at Katrina. Amethyst walked around her father over to the dragon. As she approached, with her gentle eyes looking directly into the dragon's, he began to grow calmer, allowing the girls to approach him. He was still a bit leery of humans being so close, but he understood, as Amethyst let him know they were friends.

"We won't hurt you, dragon. We can help you," Cindy said.

"What is your name?" Gia asked.

"My name is Omon, the protector of the forest," wheezed the dragon.

"My name is Gia, and these are my friends, Katrina and Cindy, and the small unicorns are Amethyst and Obsidian. Pleased to meet you."

The dragon lay back down, and Gia now walked up to his head. "Please relax. I'm going to take a look at your wing. It looks like it might need to be set," she said as she glanced at the wing that was twisted at an odd angle. "I'll try to be as careful as possible."

Since the dragon didn't respond, and didn't eat her, she assumed that she had his permission. On closer examination of the dragon's wing, Gia confirmed his wing had been broken when he landed.

"I will need all of you to help me set this dragon's wing. First, I need to have several branches from the willow tree cut off for a splint. Obsidian, could you and Cindy gather several long straight limbs, and Katrina, could you bring over the vines that have been gathered and have them ready to help bind the willow limbs onto the wing of the dragon? Amethyst, I need you to continue to calm the dragon down."

Everyone jumped to do Gia's bidding. It was as if Gia had become a general and everyone obeyed.

"Here are the limbs to make the splint for him," Cindy said, out of breath.

"Good, now I need you and Katrina to hold the limbs in place while I wrap the vines around the wing."

After completing the treatment of the dragon, Amethyst sang a soothing song, so the dragon drifted into a deep, healing sleep with the pleasant hum of a unicorn song around him. With the dragon in the presence of the girls, they heard many voices whispering and complaining.

Gia shook her head. "Do you guys hear several conversations going on at once?"

"Yes, are those all the unicorns talking?" Cindy said.

"I think so," Katrina said.

"How are we hearing all their conversations? I wonder if they know we can hear them," Gia said.

Lunar came over to the girls. "Yes, we know you can hear us. It is a special connection given when a dragon is near. Humans are able to hear what we are saying, and the connection always remains."

Moonbeam came over to speak to Gia. "Gia, the elders want to know if you are going to give them the plants you gathered to ease their pain."

"I am so sorry. Yes, I will do that right away. I got side tracked with helping the dragon and used some to treat him. Katrina and Cindy, we need more aloe vera and white willow bark. Then we need to grind up the feverfew and cat's claw flowers to prepare for the elders."

"Can't they just eat the plants and get better?" Katrina said as she yawned.

"No, for it to be the most potent, we must grind the flowers to create a pulp and place it on the willow bark and feed it to the elders, "Gia said.

After the flowers were prepared, the girls went around and served it to each of the five elders of the herd. When the girls had finished with their work, Moonbeam signaled for them to join her where she showed them some plants to eat saying, "These plants are very good and filling and will restore your strength. I am sure you are all exhausted. You have been working without stopping since we arrived in this dense forest."

After they had enjoyed the impromptu salad, Cindy said, "This has been the most unusual couple of days. First, all of you are unicorns, and then not unicorns, and then creatures attacked us from the sky that looked like dragons, but were more like pterodactyls, and then there really was a dragon, and then there's this constant bickering between Starscape and Lunar."

Moonbeam's eyes softened, and she seemed to smile.

Gia said, "May I ask you a question?"

Moonbeam's voice sounded in her head, "Certainly. You want to hear the story of Lunar and Starscape."

Gia nodded.

Chapter 14

Moonbeam smiled. "It's actually my story, too. Why don't you three make yourselves comfortable? This is a bit of a long story."

The girls sat among the soft ferns facing Moonbeam as the sun sank behind the trees in the west, and the rest of the herd started to settle for the night. Lunar could be seen patrolling around the perimeter of the herd. Obsidian and Amethyst settled in close to other girls; they too were interested in the history of their father and uncle.

A long time ago, when the unicorns roamed free in the land of majesty, when the world was young, there were pure fields of golden flowers and plains of sweet spring grass that tasted like honey citrus. In the forest, ferns carpeted the undergrowth of towering redwood trees that protected the unicorns, so they could not be easily seen. The land was full of magic and safety, and the foals would play in the clover sweet fields near the Turquoise River that lazily cut through the land. Dragons and unicorns lived in harmony guarding and protecting each other. Dragons flew above, watching for any danger from the unicorn hunters, while the unicorns gave the dragons the power of camouflage. Like a chameleon, they would instantly turn into the colors around them, so that they could not be easily seen by dragon hunters. They merely appeared as a shimmer.

Many unicorn tribes lived on the land. The two most dominant tribes were the Morningstar tribe and the Starlight tribe. In late May, Star, from the Starlight tribe, gave birth to two foals. They named the white foal Starscape and a black foal, they named Lunar. It was not very common for mares to birth twins. It was known that when twin foals were born, it was a time of great power and prosperity for the tribe. Knight was the leader of the Starlight tribe and banished the black foal and his mother from the herd. Knight believed that the black unicorn was a bad omen. He made up many stories why the black one was evil even though the stories were untrue. In reality, the black unicorn was unique and had strong powers that came from within.

The other tribes didn't agree with what Knight had done. They thought it was wrong and did not think it was appropriate to shun the mother and her foal from the herd. Star and Lunar found a valley on the outskirts of the Starlight tribe's territory and lived by themselves. The Morningstar tribe would check on them often, and when they needed help, they would provide it for Lunar and Star.

As the mother and her foal continued to live in the valley, it seemed to have a different kind of magic. The grass was a deep green with the pungent taste of sweet honey and mint mixed together with the jasmine and orange blossoms. The animals in this valley had a shimmering glow like candlelight that flickered in the wind. There was a powerful bush that was highly prized. When animals were injured or lost limbs, they would eat from this bush, and their limbs would regenerate and become even stronger than before. This bush had translucent berries that reflected the colors of the sunrise and flowers the color of pink crabapple blossoms.

There was a majestic Turquoise River painted with gigantic lily pads the size of a dinner plate with sapphire rocks by the horsetail plants hiding them. As Lunar grew, he became stronger than other unicorns, and he had a glow about him that was never seen before. He was not only physically stronger, but gained wisdom when making life decisions. Lunar became an expert in observing the world around him and using that knowledge to make wise choices. His mother also seemed to become stronger, physically and mentally. She was able to express her wisdom verbally so that others could share in what she had observed and learned. Instead of her fur becoming dull, it became sleek and shimmery. The Morningstar herd noticed this and invited them to join their tribe. Star welcomed the safety of this tribe. When she joined the tribe, she changed her name to Morning Song and became second in command of the tribe.

Many years later, a strange group of beings started to invade the land destroying the beautiful trees. They were humans and started cutting the forest's trees. Many villages started to spring up destroying more and more of the environment that was filled with magic and beauty. As the territories of the unicorn tribes shrank, the unicorns were forced to battle to defend their land. The tribes had to join their power to cause the humans to stop encroaching onto their land.

As they battled for their territory, many of the tribes disappeared. Not only was their land destroyed, the unicorns were left exposed, so that small bands of hunters could burn them out of hiding. As the unicorns came out, The Hunters used dark magic to cause them to be unable to defend themselves, and The Hunters took their horns and rendered the unicorns powerless. As a final blow, the horns gave The Hunters strong powers. As the population of unicorns decreased, The Hunters started to kill off each other to keep the power for themselves, until there was only one Hunter left. We call him, The Hunter.

By this time, there were only two unicorn tribes left, the tribe of Morningstar and the Starlight clan. They knew that they were stronger together, but there was an undercurrent of division between the two tribes because of the past when Knight had banished Star and Lunar. A few years passed, and Lunar challenged his father for the leadership of the combined herds. Knight's power had started to dim, and he didn't know that Lunar's magic and power had grown, so the battle for leadership was intense. Starscape tried to help his father, but their combined strength was less than adequate to defeat Lunar.

Knight knew he had been defeated, so he allowed Lunar to be leader. Starscape was angry because Knight had said that Starscape would be the next leader; but natural law had fallen into place, and the stronger became the leader. Now, it was time to choose a queen for the herd. Lunar remembered how I had been kind to him. At times, I would wander away from the Starlight herd to visit Star and him in the valley. I would help keep them company and enjoyed spending time with him. So that is how I became the queen of this herd.

The herds were joined, and things seemed to be going well. That is until last year. Suddenly the power of the herd started to diminish. Lunar and I couldn't determine why the power was waning. By that time, I was already pregnant with the twin foals, and I focused on their growth within me, but I knew that this had been a great concern of Lunar's especially since the land had been burning. I think that is why he feels so strongly about contacting our king.

Cindy asked while yawning, "Wait! You have a king?"

Moonbeam said quietly, looking at Gia and Katrina who were already asleep, "Shhh, I'll finish the story tomorrow night. Get some rest."

Cindy lay her head down and said, "All right," before drifting off to sleep.

The sun stretched its rays across the land. Its warmth gently awakened the sleeping herd, and each one stretched. The elders felt like yearlings and ran and jumped around the patch of land where they had camped. The dragon, too, awakened and stretched out his wings, finding that his formerly broken wing had a new strength and power to it.

"Be careful as you stretch your wing that was broken. It may not be completely healed yet," Gia said.

"My wing feels so strong. I can feel the strength coming back and look," the young dragon said, peering at the wing, "The splints and vines have disappeared during the night. I can move it. It will let me lift off to fly," said Omon.

Soaring up from the ground through the broken branches, he was able to fly high above the forest. Coming back down from his flight, he reported that he saw a beautiful valley, glowing with life and magic.

"Should I fly ahead and check the land?"

"Do you see a path from the sky that leads the way?" Katrina asked.

"No, I just see the valley from above."

"Over here is a path that is lit." Pointing in the direction that was lit. She asked, "Is the valley in this direction?"

Omon replied that it was.

"Then, this is what we shall follow to the valley," Katrina said.

"Could you estimate how far away the land is from your bird's eye view?" Lunar asked.

"I would figure it would be about a day's more journey," Omon said.

"Okay, let's get moving so we can arrive at the valley by evening," Moonbeam said.

Katrina and Amethyst were at the head with Cindy and Obsidian nearby in the group traveling along the path. Gia traveled close to Moonbeam with the elders in the middle, and, as usual, Lunar acted as the rear guard. Now, they had an addition to their group. Omon, the dragon, flew above the trees watching from the sky for any danger that might come to the herd.

Chapter 15

As the herd settled for the night, the girls and the foals settled down next to Moonbeam, excited to hear the next part of the story.

"Where was I? Oh yes, I remember. I was telling you about why Lunar feels so strongly about contacting King Aaron."

Cindy asked, "Wait a minute. Who is Aaron? That sounds like a human name?" Moonbeam shook her head. "Oh, I forgot that you don't know about Aaron. Let me go back a bit and tell you about how we found him."

One day, Lunar and his mother were grazing in a field painted with wildflowers in an array of rainbow colors with the dominant colors of lavender and yellow. They came upon a little pond they had never seen before. The water was like crystal, and it shimmered in the light. As they looked into the pond, they noticed a shiny golden chain with an amethyst unicorn.

Lunar heard a quiet gentle voice speaking in his head while he was looking at the talisman. He turned to his mother and asked, "Mom, do you hear a gentle voice talking to us?"

His mother told him, "No."

Before they could say anything more, the water started to form into a young human child. As the water continued to churn and boil, a boy appeared from the water. He stepped out of the water and turned toward them.

They ran from the boy and bumped into me.

"What are you running from?" I asked them.

"Do you not see the little boy standing in the field? He's peeking through the huge ferns," Star asked.

"Why yes, I have seen him a few times," I said. "I like to watch him as he plays and explores this part of the valley."

"Is he dangerous?" Star asked.

"No, I haven't seen him do anything but sit today. A few days ago, I saw him pick up a bird that had a broken wing. He collected some flowers and a stick, and splinted the wing, so it would be held steady. Then he disappeared, and when he came back, he had released the bird, and it was strong again. On other occasions, I have seen how he is gentle with many of the creatures in the valley," I told her.

Lunar twitched his ears again, as if he was trying to be rid of an annoying buzz.

I noticed that and asked him "Why are you twitching your ears so much? I don't see any bugs around your ears."

He said, "I keep hearing a whisper like a gentle breeze in my ears."

"Look at the child. He is looking in this direction."

"Hello. I won't hurt you. I'd like to see who I am feeling," the small boy said.

Again, Lunar shook his ears.

"What is going on?" I asked.

"I think the child was trying to communicate with him before we ran away," Star said. "Lunar said he had heard a gentle voice."

I said, "How cool is that! Why don't you answer him, Lunar?"

"I'm not sure it is safe," Lunar said.

"You may not have to show yourself. Just think in your mind," I suggested.

"Have humans spoken to us before?" he asked me.

"It is rare, but I remember hearing stories from hundreds of years ago about humans communicating with us," Star said.

"Hello, my name is Aaron. I want to be your friend. Please let me see who you are," came the voice in Lunar's head.

"I am Lunar. Why are you in our land?" Lunar said in his head as he turned to look where the small boy stood.

Aaron jumped as he heard the voice in his head.

"Hello Lunar. I like to come here because I enjoy the quiet. I like to come visit the animals here also."

"Where do you live?"

"At 2274 Wonderland Road, in Colorado."

"Lunar, will you come out from the trees, so I can see you?"

Lunar poked his head out from the ferns he was behind. The trees were still behind him.

"A unicorn! You are a unicorn!" Aaron said out loud. "I didn't know unicorns were real. Does that mean there are also dragons and Pegusi that are real?"

"I can't tell you that because the strong magic that used to be in this land has faded away as the last of the unicorns are being hunted and destroyed by the Evil Hunter who has been growing in power over the last several years in our land," Lunar spoke in his mind.

"Can I help you?"

"I am afraid not. You are welcome to come into this valley, but you must not wander into the woods. The Hunter will eat you if he knows you are here."

"I must leave now. My parents are calling for me."

"Bye, Aaron."

"Bye Lunar. I will visit again soon."

And with that, the boy disappeared back into the ferns, and Lunar did not hear from him again. For many days, Lunar would come to the place where he met Aaron but was confused because Aaron did not return.

Chapter 16

Then one day, Lunar heard a faint cry. He knew it was Aaron but didn't know where the cry was coming from.

"I am scared. I don't know where I am. I have tubes all over my body, but the lights are dimming. I hear my Mom and Dad moaning, but I can't reach my hand out to them. I can't move. What is happening to me?"

Aaron grasped the unicorn charm in his hands. Then with a searing pain, the charm was taken from his hands, and as a flash of light jumped into his vision, he felt himself falling, sinking into the ground. Soil covered his body as he was laid deep into the earth. He heard the cries of his mother and father as he sank deeper into the ground.

Lunar could feel what Aaron was feeling and called out to Star and me.

"Help me get hold of the spirit of Aaron. He is fading. I am not sure I can help him."

As we touched our horns together, the earth began to shake like roaring thunder. Flashes of light surrounded us as a pond started to appear with a bubbling, gurgling sound. The water formed the body of Aaron. As the magic danced across the sky, Aaron landed hard on the ground next to us.

"Aaron, Aaron, what has happened to you?" Lunar asked.

I laid my head on Aaron's chest and a purplish glow encircled his body. As the light faded, Star placed her horn on Aaron's eyes. They fluttered open and then closed again. The sun passed overhead at noon. Aaron sat up with blurred vision. As his vision cleared, he was looking at three sets of gentle, concerned eyes looking into his.

"Lunar, how did I get here? The last thing I remember was being in the hospital with tubes all over my body. I couldn't breathe. I had the flu really bad. Then I was covered in dirt, sinking deeper into the earth."

"I heard you cry out to me. I knew I needed to rescue you from whatever pain you were going through. I needed my mom and my friend, Moonbeam, to help me rescue you."

"Will I ever be able to get back home?"

"I don't think so. You have passed away from that life. You must let go of the old life and embrace the renewed life that you have been given."

Suddenly I lifted my head, "Oh, no." I heard Knight calling for me. I didn't realize how long I had been gone. I dashed off into Starlight territory where I was punished for being gone for so long. I was forced to stay in the middle of the herd as we traveled for the next three days, so I was not able to see how Aaron was cared for by Lunar and Star.

Cindy said with tears in her eyes, "That's such a terribly sad story. Are there other children who have passed away on earth and come here?" Then a terrible thought came to her. "Is that what's happened to us?"

Moonbeam smiled and shook her head. "No, you three are not dead in the other world. I'm not sure why you're here, but your life spirit is different from when Aaron first arrived, and no, there are no other children who have arrived as Aaron did. He has grown up in our land and is very helpful to the unicorns and dragons."

Katrina asked, "Where is Aaron now?"

Moonbeam continued with her story.

Aaron grew up beside Lunar and Star, and over the years, he grew in strength and power. As he matured, he traveled this land and discovered many things. The most important was the discovery of the Everberry bush. He found that if the unicorns ate the berries and leaves of this plant, their magic and strength increased.

Then one day, Aaron was captured by The Hunter and was imprisoned for many days. During that time, Aaron became very weak. He told The Hunter that he needed everberries to eat, and The Hunter learned that these plants also sustained the unicorn's power. That was when The Hunter decided to destroy all of these plants, but he kept one alive for himself.

The largest Everberry bush was in the valley of the Turquoise River. The Hunter dug up the bush and carried it to his camp. He replanted it and forced Aaron to cultivate the plant, so it grew strong and secure in its new place. As time passed, The Hunter realized that the unicorns were becoming weaker. He relished the thought of putting an end to all the unicorn tribes.

Then one night, Lunar helped Aaron escape, and as they were leaving, Aaron collected the seeds and berries from the Everberry plant, so they would be able to repopulate the land with the plants. Lunar led Aaron to a secret place that The Hunter didn't know about, and as Aaron continued to grow into a young man, he developed the area and worked on cultivating the plants.

During this time, The Hunter destroyed all the unicorn herds except for the last two tribes--the tribes of the Night Sky and the Morning Star. The two tribes knew they would be safer with larger numbers, but they also had divisions and continued to shun Lunar. Lunar ended up having to challenge his father in order to unite the tribes. He defeated his father and became the leader of the combined clan. His brother, Starscape, despised Lunar for defeating their father and taking over the herd that Starscape's father had said would pass down to him. Lunar chose me to be his mate and co leader

And now you have the history of the unicorns of the valley.

"Wow what an interesting history the unicorns have had," Gia said.

"I can't believe how cruel and evil The Hunter has become," Katrina said.

"The story about Aaron is very strange and scary because it is so inline with my own family story. The address 2274 Wonderland Rd. is, or was, my address before the fire destroyed my home," said Cindy.

The girls wanted to think about the story Moonbeam had told them, but before they could begin to ponder its implications, they were all in deep slumber.

The next evening, the herd arrived at a huge dark tree trunk. It looked like the tree the girls had come through before meeting the unicorns. Katrina led the way through the tree to a beautiful hidden valley with a Turquoise River flowing with the scent of a new spring day. This valley was filled with magic and was a peaceful place for recovery for the unicorns after a challenging journey.

As they had traveled from the desolation of the destroyed land of The Hunter, the brightness of the white coats continued to turn into an even darker gray. Only Amethyst's coat remained white. Preparing the concoction to restore the horns of the unicorns became the ultimate goal for everyone. They only had four days left before the unicorns would permanently become horses.

Lunar said, "This is a magical valley. I know that all the ingredients should be here--pussy willow, horsetail, lily pads, rocks called dragon tears, and, the final ingredient would be the Everberry bush with translucent berries and flowers the color of pink crabapple blossoms."

They searched the area for the supplies needed to regenerate unicorn horns. They found all the ingredients for the potion except for the most powerful one. The Everberry bush. Lunar continued to search, but he could not find the Everberry bush. He then came across an area that seemed to be inky black with the smell of rot and death that assaulted his nose with sticky slime and mold. It seemed to be creeping out of the corner of the valley. In order to stop the spread of this mold, he used his horn to trap the slime from progressing any further. Cindy was exploring the other side of the valley when she sensed an anguished cry from Lunar.

"The Everberry bush has been destroyed."

"What do you mean?" she mindspoke in her mind to Lunar.

"Come over to where I am and look."

Cindy quickly sprinted to where Lunar was standing and from several feet away from him, her nose was scorched with the acrid stench of rot and death. Covering her nose, she rushed over and saw the appalling sight of mold and black slime, but she also noticed where the soil had been dug up.

"The plant has not been destroyed. It has been transported and replanted somewhere else," Obsidian said, pointing his horn at the hole. His head perked up as he spoke. He stared across the Turquoise River. In his mind's eye, he saw a vision of the Everberry bush a two days' journey from the valley. He told them what he had seen.

"I have seen where the Everberry bush has been taken. It is near The Hunter's camp. Cindy and I will leave immediately. It will be at least a two day journey."

Gia overheard the conversation and quickly gathered some plants that she knew would increase the strength of both Cindy and Obsidian.

"Here are some herbs that will give you strength for your journey. There should be berries along the way that you can eat."

Obsidian said, "I will watch over Cindy and make certain that she only eats plants that will provide her with nourishment. No harm will come to her. She must do great things in a very short time."

Cindy's eyes opened widely. "What do you mean by that?" she asked loudly.

Gia ignored her outburst. "Go quickly now," she said. "Time is running short for the herd.

The herbs were bitter in taste, but as they ate, they felt an empowering strength fill their muscles. The quickest route to the camp would be to cross the Turquoise River. Feeling emboldened, Obsidian and Cindy entered the river. The river was icy cold and took Cindy's breath away. She put her arm around Obsidian's neck and held tightly, but as the pair moved into the center of the river, the current took hold and pulled them apart.

Obsidian, being the lighter of the two, was quickly pulled ahead of Cindy and moved further down the river.

Cindy called out to him in her mind. "Obsidian! Are you alright? Can you swim?"

Obsidian responded. "I seem to be able to. Quickly, swim to the other side! I'll meet you there!

Chapter 17

The current increased in speed, and Cindy lost sight of the young unicorn. Now, she was concerned for her own safety. She was grateful that she knew how to swim and that she had taken a class on how to survive falling into a swollen river back in Colorado. Now, she knew why so many people drowned in the spring in swollen rivers. She was able to turn her body so that her feet were headed downstream, and she moved her arms whenever she felt the current lessen, until she found herself on a sandbar on the side of the river.

As she pulled herself from the icy water, she flopped onto the grass at the river's edge and tried to contact Obsidian. "Obsidian! Where are you? Can you hear me?"

There was a long moment of silence. Then to Cindy's ultimate joy, there was a response, although it sounded weak. "I have made it across the river, but I need to rest for a while. I am not hurt though. How are you?"

"I feel the same," said Cindy. "I'm lying in the grass looking at a cloud in the sky that looks like a rabbit chasing a hawk."

"I see that same cloud," said Obsidian. "Let's rest for a bit and then try to find each other so that we can continue our journey.

Cindy sat up after several minutes and said, "How are you doing now?"

Obsidian mindspoke and replied, "Much better. I can stand now and am nibbling on some of this delicious green grass."

Cindy groaned. "The grass around me doesn't look delicious at all. I wish I had a peanut butter and jelly sandwich, or better yet, one of Katrina's paninis.

There was silence from Obsidian. I do not know what a panini is. Is it a plant of some kind?"

Cindy laughed, "No, it's a pocket of plants that have been cooked filled with other plants that are then heated."

Obsidian was silent again. "Why not just eat the plants?"

Cindy laughed again. "Maybe we should try to find each other. I saw you go further down the river than I went. How about if I start walking down the river and you walk upstream?" If we mindspeak to each other and tell each other what we're seeing, we should be able to find each other fairly easily."

Obsidian thought that was a great idea and added, "Be sure to stay away from the river's edge!"

As they hit the other side, their legs felt like they were walking even though they were running. The trip went twice as fast because of the herbs. A day later, Cindy and Obsidian were at the edge of a pine forest with the scent of vanilla drifting through the air, mixed with the subtle scent of roses from the bushes that were growing around the pine trees. They settled for a short break to regain their strength. Cindy climbed a nearby boulder to see what the path ahead held for them. Her eyes were assaulted by a bright golden light. She climbed down the rock and called to Obsidian to tell him what she'd seen.

She felt pulled by the light as she walked across a field of wildflowers, almost as if she was in a trance. In the center of the field, she saw the purest Everberry bush alone in the distance giving off the light. It was so bright! The colors swirled into ribbons of pink and purple. As she continued to move closer, her eyes were drawn to a golden scaled unicorn with a horn four feet long and a tail of golden strands of hair blowing in the breeze that was also stirring up amethyst flowers from the Everberry bush.

Obsidian felt that this wasn't a safe place and spoke with his mind to Cindy. "Cindy! No! Don't trust that creature!"

"This creature seems gentle; it hasn't attacked us yet."

Cindy, believing that the creature before her was friendly, rushed over to reach out and touch one of the amethyst flowers, but the creature quickly blocked her from the plant. Cindy stepped back away from the plant saying, "I'm sorry. I should have asked to touch the flowers."

"What do you want, young one?" uttered the unicorn creature.

"We need to have some of the Everberry plant. There is a group of unicorns who need to have their horns restored. An evil creature has sawed off all the horns of the unicorns. We have only three days before all their magic will be gone, and they will only be horses."

"You lie! The unicorn with you has a horn. You want the power of this plant for yourself!"

Obsidian stepped forward and said, "My twin and I were born shortly after my mother's horn was taken from her. The herd is over by the Turquoise River, a two day journey from here where the plant you are protecting was taken from by the evil being with the jagged scar down his back that our leader gave him years ago."

Rolling across the wind came the acrid smell of burnt rotting flesh and a pounding and rattling of chains that invaded their nose and ears as the scaled unicorn let out a hideous laugh. "You must mean my Master!"

A chain net suddenly flew over them from behind, and they were captured. It landed on top of them, and they were securely encased; they were like a gift bag. Cindy and Obsidian turned to see their enemy.

The Hunter laughed again. "Thank you, Uniscale, for this wonderful present."

"Master, did you know there is another unicorn with a horn in the herd. This black one's twin sister is there."

"I thought I felt a stronger power flowing in the wind. We will go tomorrow and claim that power for ourselves. Come now, let's celebrate this capture of the leader of the pure ones. We will defeat the unicorns forever. Let us prepare for our journey."

The Hunter and Uniscale left the meadow and walked toward a cave at the edge of the forest. Obsidian and Cindy both turned to see the entrance that was hidden in shadow. They tried to lift the edge of the net, but it was weighted in such a way that it was impossible to move it from the ground. They could walk a short distance under the net, but they were most definitely trapped. They could see the Everberry bush, but even pushing against the net, they couldn't quite reach it, and Cindy cried out in frustration. Obsidian attempted to cut through the chains with his horn, but The Hunter had reinforced the metal with the magic from the unicorn horns he wore in the abominable necklace.

As night fell, Cindy tried to mind speak with Lunar to warn him that The Hunter was coming. She couldn't connect with him due to some interference.

"Who are you? How did you get here?"

A different voice was coming to her mind, and it confused her.

"Get out of my head! I need to contact Lunar. His herd is in danger!"

"Lunar, the black unicorn?"

"Yes, now get out of my mind!" Cindy mind spoke.

"I know him. Let me help."

"How do you know him?"

"I used to visit him when I was little with a charm that allowed me to move between two different worlds."

"You mean this charm I have, you had before me."

"What does it look like?"

"It is a black unicorn with a golden horn. My mom gave it to me many years ago when I was five. She said it was a special charm, and she remembered how my older brother loved it and claimed it was magic, and he could travel to a land with unicorns and dragons."

Cindy couldn't believe that she was mindspeaking with a stranger and telling him all these details. Her mom always told her that she couldn't stop talking when she was under stress.

"I thought I would never see it again. Lunar must have used the connection to call you here; that charm had power in this land, and you can use it to escape from the Hunter."

"Who are you?"

"I am Aaron, son of Alexander McCullum Hanson. I have been in this world for many years. I have been working to protect the unicorns, but I have failed miserably.

The Hunter has grown in power with every herd that he has destroyed!" came the reply in her head.

"Alexander Hanson? Really? Can you help me and Obsidian escape? We need to gather some Everberry leaves, flowers and berries to save the unicorns."

"I know where you are. I have been moving toward you as we have been communicating, but I am still a ways from you. Place your hands and charm onto Obsidian's horn and hold tight."

Following the directions, she wrapped her hands and charm around the horn. As she held her hands there, she felt a burning sensation. She held tight. The chains silently dropped to the ground. Letting go of the horn, in an instant, the two prisoners ran past the Everberry bush and toward the forest. Uniscale turned in time to see her get out of the net. With a mighty roar, Uniscale charged after her.

From a few yards away, a tall thin young man shouted, "Jump on the foal and run!"

As Obsidian dashed toward the woods, Cindy fell off. The Hunter sped over to her, grabbed her leg and started to drag her back. Aaron ran over and used a sword to chop off the hand of The Hunter. Aaron lifted Cindy into his arms and with a flash of light transported her into the woods.

Uniscale was blinded briefly and was left confused. It turned toward its master and saw that he was injured. Uniscale bit off some leaves and everberries and, bringing them to the master, worked them into a mush and spat them onto the stump of the master's hand. Immediately, it regenerated into a scaled hand with bulging muscles. As his hand grew back, The Hunter became much stronger.

"Who was that, Uniscale?" He looked like a human, but there haven't been humans here for years."

"I don't know. He appeared out of nowhere and then evaporated into the woods with the girl and the foal."

Chapter 18

Aaron, Cindy and Obsidian arrived in a house made of stone. Inside the humbly furnished home was a picture on the mantle of the fireplace of a freckle-faced boy in the arms of Cindy's father and her mother holding her as a baby. The boy was wearing a charm around his neck identical to the one that was in her hand.

Cindy's mind spun with many questions. Who really was this young man? Where were they? How did they get wherever they were? Then she decided that only a couple questions were most important for the moment, and the rest could be answered later.

"Where did you get those pictures? How did they come to you?" Cindy asked.

"When I arrived here, they were tucked into the suit pocket that I was wearing when I was buried after an extended stay at the hospital."

Cindy turned to the young man. "Are you King Aaron?"

The young man smiled. "You must have been talking to Moonbeam."

Cindy said, "My father's name is also Alexander Hanson. I'm the baby in that picture and those are my parents, too."

"I have missed them very much. How are they doing?" Aaron asked.

Cindy took a deep breath, trying to comprehend everything that was happening so quickly around her. Finally she said, "They are doing fine. Mom remembers you with a slight smile whenever she says your name. She sometimes looks far away, but she remembers the good times. Dad doesn't talk about you much. I think he still misses you a lot. He doesn't even care that I have been with him for ten years. He constantly bemoans the fact that I am a girl and not a boy," Cindy said as she walked around the small house.

Suddenly, she turned away from reminiscing about the past and her family and turned her focus back to the unicorns.

"We only have two days before the herd will all become horses. We need to get moving. It is a two day journey from where The Hunter took us, and I have no idea how far away we are now from the herd. If we don't get there by tomorrow, the unicorns will be extinct, and we still need to get the Everberry to complete the remedy."

"Come. Follow me. I have cultivated an Everberry bush for the past five years," said Aaron, leading Cindy and Obsidian to a small courtyard behind the stone house.

"But it has pale pink, almost white flowers. I don't see any translucent berries or amethyst colored leaves. Lunar said we need to find the purest white flowers. We need to go back to The Hunter's bush. That is the only kind that will work," Cindy cried.

"We cannot go back to The Hunter's hideout. We don't have time," Aaron said, as he started gathering the leaves, flowers and berries from the bush in his garden. "Where is Lunar's herd staying?"

"By the Turquoise River, but I am afraid. The Hunter knows where it is, because he stole the purest Everberry bush from there."

"No need to worry. We can get there quickly," Aaron said.

He gave a shrill whistle and down from the sky dove a Pegasus with wings as clear as glass. It landed and with a snort of fairy dust onto the black foal, Obsidian grew lovely blue wings.

This is Splendor. She is my guardian mother. She raised me in this world after I died in your world. We have no time to lose. Let's soar to the Turquoise River.

Cindy jumped onto Obsidian, and in a flash of light, they were high in the air and in another flash of light, they were above the river. Cindy and Obsidian circled around behind her friends to surprise them before landing.

Chapter 19

For the past three days, Lunar had been trying to connect with Cindy. The herd was on the ninth day since The Hunter had sawed off Moonbeam's horn. The only unicorns left with horns were Amethyst and Lunar.

Lunar worried, "She should be back by now. What has happened to her? Is she alive? Cindy, where are you?"

Suddenly, he was pulled from his worry about Cindy, and his horn started to glow as he looked across the Turquoise River.

He began to panic. "The Hunter is on his way!"

"How far away is he?" Starscape asked.

"He is about a day's journey away. We need to come up with a plan. We cannot let him get hold of Amethyst or the girls. Our hope is in them."

Moonbeam suddenly whinnied. She felt a strong power burning within her heart that she hadn't felt for years. There was a great break in the sky, and a golden streak of light snapped across it that ended in crystal embers like fireworks that poured into the Turquoise River. She heard a splash of hooves colliding with water. Running to the river with a quivering of her nose, the smell of orange blossoms and lavender penetrated through the air, refreshing, like the first snow of the season. The freshness of the scent washed over her body and a tingling sensation rose on her back like pine needles brushing against her back.

Splendor, Moonbeam's adopted sister had returned, and on her back was King Aaron. A musical song erupted from the unicorns as they saw the painting of colors lighting up the sky like the northern lights. As Splendor moved closer, King Aaron dismounted and walked toward Lunar. Unicorns bowed as he walked by.

"Greetings, my friends, the last of the unicorns. We must join our powers to restore our strength and become strong again. I feel a new power, a new glow. The unity that has been absent for many years has returned. Who is responsible for the return to unity?" Aaron asked. The herd parted as Katrina, Gia and Lunar came forward.

"We did not bring unity back. We reminded them that to accomplish power, one must learn to celebrate one's differences; not to shun those who are different from us, but to see the gifts each member brings to the tribe," Gia said.

Gia and Katrina parted again and behind them, Amethyst rested

"We have also been shown that trust and kindness intertwined like her horn of silver and gold create a beautiful power that has diffused among the tribe. This unicorn has only shown kindness and acceptance and has encouraged us all to set aside our differences and show love and let peace overwhelm us with a new life of unity and peace," Lunar said.

"But we have lost our best friend as she and Obsidian sacrificed their safety to search for the Everberry bush that will restore the horns of our unicorn friends. We have only one day left before the unicorns will be gone forever. We have been working to create a medicine that will regenerate the mighty horns of the unicorn," Gia said sadly.

While everyone's attention had been focused on Splendor and King Aaron, Cindy and Obsidian had landed behind the group. They had heard this speech as they quietly circled behind Gia and Katrina. As they approached, Gia felt a tickling sensation on the back of her neck and with a snort, Obsidian blew pink flowers from his nose. As Katrina jumped, Gia screamed.

"Boo! Surprise! I am here!" Cindy said.

Katrina and Gia turned around as tears of joy poured out of their eyes. They hugged Cindy. Obsidian and Amethyst trotted over to each other and with a clashing of their horns an amazing show of purple, pink and golden sparks flew overhead.

"I hate to disrupt this joyous reunion, but our enemy is nearly upon us," Starscape said.

Lunar called for the girls, "Come, we have much work to do."

Cindy, Katrina and Gia moved within the camp gathering pussywillows, horsetails, lily pads and dragon tear gems.

"How much of this material do we need to blend together and create this medicine?" Gia asked.

"I know what needs to be collected. I have made this medicine before, but I was not able to complete the process until it was too late for the disappearing unicorn herds," Aaron said.

"What parts of these plants do we need?" Cindy asked.

"From the pussywillow, we need to pluck off the fuzzy buds of the plant and the leaves. From the horsetails, we need to harvest the whole plant, especially the top brown part and the leaves closest to the water and under the water around the roots of the plant. You will find gems that are a deep blue like sapphire underneath the plant. We will need forty of them. To improve the smell, we will need to collect mint leaves and lilac flowers," Aaron explained.

"What are we to mix it in, and we still don't have the Everberry bush," Gia said. Moonbeam and Splendor walked to the center of the camp and together they created a fire As the smoke rose, Gia and Cindy began to panic as the smell of charred wood permeated through the air. The smell of the blazing wildfire flashed into their memories from the fire that they had to escape that devoured their homes back in Colorado. Breaking out in cold sweats, they collapsed on the ground as their hearts pounded, and they screamed because of the pictures of the ferocious fire consuming all that was in its path that controlled their minds. Obsidian, Amethyst, Moonbeam and Splendor dashed over to the girls with Splendor's wings creating a shower of gold dust covering the girls' minds. The foals touched their horns together and a soothing aura encased the girls, and their breathing slowed. A tranquil sleep came down upon them.

Aaron placed his hand on his sister's head. He wanted to know what had just happened. When he placed his hand upon her, he saw the terrible trauma that was going through her mind like a movie. Terrified by the sights of fear that showed in Aaron's eyes, Lunar broke the connection.

"What just happened to my friends? Did they just have an allergic reaction from the Horsetail dust?" Katrina cried.

Aaron shook his head as he moved toward Katrina and said, "They have had a terrible experience with a fire that destroyed their home."

"You mean that they have no house to return to? I didn't know that the wildfires had completely destroyed their houses."

"Look, they are getting up and gathering the materials they dropped. Let's not say anything about this for now," Aaron said.

Katrina ran back over to where they were gathering the last of the ingredients for the remedy. She helped them bring the materials to Aaron. No one said anything about what had just happened.

"What are we to place them in?" Gia asked.

"I have a large pot to place them in. I want you and Cindy to stay close to the foals. Katrina, help me bring this pot to the fire," said Aaron.

Lunar, who stood next to Aaron asked, "Where are the ingredients from the Everberry bush?"

"I have the parts we need right over here. The everberries, flowers and leaves go in after the mixture has started to boil."

"Katrina, I need you to stir the liquid until it is thick like honey," said Aaron. "Lunar, come with me. I will show you the parts of the Everberry plant I have been cultivating for many years. It has grown nicely."

Lunar said, "This is not the right plant. The berries are not pure white. There are too many imperfections of tints of pink on the flowers. I don't see any translucent berries either and the leaves are not lavender. They are dark purple."

Aaron said, "Trust me. This will work. I have experimented with this plant. I have been able to use it to regenerate limbs of trees and wings of birds many times. I have had to repair other creatures' wings, legs and arms. Now, I need to bring these to the fire. I smell that the lilac and mint are drifting through the air. The concoction should be ready to boil."

Just as Aaron got to the pot, the liquid started to boil, forming into a thick gravy like texture. As he added the Everberry flowers, leaves and berries to the pot, the liquid turned to a subtle pink. As Aaron took over the stirring, he called Amethyst over. He spoke quietly to the foal. "I need you to place your horn in this mixture to change the color from pink to white."

The horn acted just like a straw and sucked all the pink coloring out, leaving the mixture a pure white.

"Thank you, Amethyst. Now, we need to let the potion cool overnight. At first light, it will be ready to apply the cream to the foreheads of the unicorns, and their horns should grow back."

Chapter 20

During the early evening, the girls gathered round the pot of the remedy to regenerate the horns of the unicorns. Not liking it in the middle of them, they moved it to a flat rock by the forest, so they could see each other better.

"Cindy, where did you find Aaron? He is so handsome. Did you know he was a king?" Katrina said.

"He actually helped me escape from The Hunter; he's so evil! I was tricked by a beautiful dragon scaled unicorn I thought was a friend that was sitting by an Everberry bush. It was so beautiful and seemed nice. I assumed, since it had both dragon and unicorn characteristics, it would be friendly. I ignored Obsidian, when he told me not to go near the creature. I went anyway, not trusting him. As soon as I reached to touch the bush, the beautiful creature turned feral and jumped in front of the bush. Before I knew it, a net had trapped Obsidian and me."

"How did he help you escape? Did he dash in like a knight in shining armor to rescue a princess from the clutches of an evil enemy?" Katrina said.

"No, I was trying to warn Lunar that The Hunter was coming, but my connection kept getting interrupted because my brother was interfering, so I couldn't get to Lunar."

"Wait! Aaron is your brother? I never knew you had a brother," Katrina said.

"I didn't think he was alive. He was five when I was born. Then at age seven, he died from leukemia. My dad still bemoans the fact I am a girl and not a boy. For the past several years, I have been trying to get him to want to spend time with me, but every time he tells me to leave, or if I mess up, he says, 'Aaron wouldn't have done that.'"

"Wow! What a horrible way to treat a daughter," Gia said.

"So, what was it like to meet your brother? Are you happy to have met him or are you wishing he wasn't alive?" Katrina asked.

"I'm not sure how I feel. I was stunned he was alive. I really haven't had much time to think about it. This day has been full of so many surprises and so much stress. I am afraid I don't know what it will be like when I go home and know my brother is alive, but I'm not sure if I'd like it if he would come back with us, or if he even can. I do know I'm glad that he's alive."

Gia looked across the camp and saw Aaron crossing over to them.

"He is coming this way," Gia said.

"Hey girls. How are you all doing? It looks like I may have interrupted some deep conversation. I am guessing that you know that I am Cindy's brother."

Gia and Katrina nodded their heads. Aaron smiled at them.

"Gia, at first light, you will want to apply the cream to the forehead of each unicorn. It may take a few hours for their horns to fully form," he instructed.

"How much cream do I put on each horn stump?"

"The size of your hand. Do not rub it in. Just put it on, like paste to paper."

"Aren't you going to be here to help?"

"No, this is where your power shines. Splendor and I have to destroy The Hunter, so the unicorns will be safe."

"But Aaron, you just got here. Why do you need to leave right now? Why can't you wait until morning?" Cindy said.

"The Hunter will be here soon. I need to stop him from getting here before you have time to help the unicorns." He whistled and Splendor flew down and landed beside him.

Gia and Katrina marveled at the magnificent Pegasus that pawed the ground in front of them. Then before they had a chance to even reach out a hand and touch her crystalline wing, Aaron leapt onto her back.

"I'll see you all soon." They headed up into the sky with a flash of lightning. They were out of sight and heading to battle The Hunter before Cindy even had a chance to say good-bye or wish him luck.

The girls were exhausted after all that had happened and, even with the best of intentions, soon all three had fallen asleep.

Uniscale had watched as once again there was a break in the sky and a golden streak of light snapped across it. It ended in crystal embers that slid into the Turquoise River. It knew that now all it had to do was wait. The Hunter commanded Uniscale to steal the formula, so the unicorns would remain as horses for the rest of their lives. Even from a distance, Uniscale could sense that the girls were fast asleep and wanted to make sure that they stayed asleep. It placed a spell on them to cause them an even deeper sleep before it went to steal the potion. Approaching the camp, it also wanted to make sure to be unseen, and so caused the deep sleep to fall on all the others.

Omon and Starscape came back from a brief walk and noticed the camp was unusually quiet. Rushing back to see what had happened, they saw that the potion had been taken. Omon let out a loud roar, and with the breath of heat coming from his mouth, he awoke the entire herd. Starscape ran over to where the foals and the girls were still sleeping. He nudged Amethyst awake, and she and Obsidian's horns tapped and the girls awakened in alarm. They realized the formula was gone.

"What has happened to the pot? Who took it?" Gia yelled.

Looking around the camp, she saw the prints of a dragon. Thinking Omon had stolen it, she charged over to him, but before she got to him, he was already flying in the air. As she realized that the prints were heading into the woods, she jumped on Starscape.

Startling the poor unicorn, he reared. Gia held onto his mane calming him, explaining to him, "We need to find who took the potion. I saw some tracks heading into the woods. We have about four hours before first light. Katrina! Cindy! We need to find the formula."

Cindy and Katrina ran into the woods. As they moved forward, they saw the trail of Uniscale and ran after it. With the power from the foals, they were able to catch up to Uniscale, faster than Gia, but when Uniscale turned, they felt a freezing blast that froze them in place.

From the sky, Omon saw that the girls were frozen, and he quickly blew fire from his nose and was able to melt the ice. Katrina and Cindy were stiff from being frozen and, at first, began to move sluggishly. Then, they continued to chase after Uniscale. Omon was on the lookout for an opportunity to grab the pot from Uniscale. Uniscale set down the pot to freeze the girls again. Omon swept down from the sky and grabbed the pot and took off into the sky. Uniscale bellowed and attempted to follow Omon and the pot that contained the potion that would regenerate the horns of the unicorns. It knew that The Hunter would be most displeased with this failure.

Just as the sun started to peak over the horizon, Omon spotted Gia on Starscape's back and landed by them. He encouraged Gia to climb off Starscape and onto his back, so they could quickly return to camp, getting there right at daybreak. They arrived in camp and were able to apply the cream to the horn stumps of all the unicorns. When it was applied, little buds of horns started to grow back immediately. Once the horns of the unicorns started growing back Uniscale was set free from the curse The Hunter had put on her.

Starscape caught up to Katrina, Cindy, and the foals as they came upon Uniscale with its scaled back towards them. A horrendous moan escaped it, and the scales started to peel off. With a tortuous rip, the scales peeled to display an undercoat of white with tints of purple that started to appear. Starscape ran over to the creature and called out to Amethyst to come quickly.

"We need to help this poor creature! I am not sure what it is, but I just know we need to help it," Starscape said.

Starscape moved closer and closer to this creature as screeching penetrated his ears and caused them to ring. Even so, he walked around and sniffed the creature. The scent seemed familiar, but he couldn't place where he had smelled it before. As the scales peeled off, and the coat began to glisten, he noticed the horn was like a silver shining star that cast glimmers of star light around him.

As its light burst into richness, he heard a voice saying, "Starscape, my son, how glad I am to see you! How is your brother Lunar? Is he still alive?"

"He is," Starscape said.

Amethyst started to move closer to the creature when Katrina saw a bright glow start to form around it. She knew that the creature was safe and moved closer to touch the undercoat.

"Stop Katrina! This creature is evil! It attacked me when I was at The Hunter's camp," Cindy said.

"Nonsense. It has a glowing light of purple shining around it, and Amethyst also knows it's safe to approach this creature," Katrina said.

"No it doesn't," Cindy said as she hid behind a tree.

"Don't be silly; it is perfectly safe."

As Katrina touched Uniscale's white coat, a stinging sensation moved through her hand just like when she first touched Amethyst. Then words began to enter her mind.

"I am the first unicorn that The Hunter caught. We need to rush to aid Aaron in battle. He is in grave danger! Quickly!"

"Cindy, call Lunar. We need to aid Aaron in battle," said Katrina.

"Lunar, Aaron needs help! How far away is he from camp?" Cindy mindspoke.

"How do you know this?" came Lunar's reply.

"The first unicorn that The Hunter caught has told us," Cindy mindspoke to him. "Quickly Lunar, we need to get to Aaron. We will explain later.

Lunar concentrated hard. He honed in on Aaron and saw a picture in his mind of how The Hunter had grown massively in power and strength. Lunar let out a loud whinny as he saw The Hunter. Terrified, he quickly estimated the distance between the camp and the battle.

Wanting to get the picture out of his mind, he focused on where Cindy was, and told her, "He is about four miles north of our camp. I will send Omon to guide you. The horns are starting to grow back, and Gia just placed the last paste onto Moonbeam's head."

Chapter 21

Aaron charged into the meadow by The Hunter's camp with Splendor. His sword was gallantly raised, poised to attack The Hunter. As Aaron closed in on The Hunter, he realized that the evil-doer had gained much power since the last time he had confronted him. He had grown double his original height, and his body had become covered in scales that were thick as bricks and across his chest, he wore a shirt made out of the horns of unicorns.

"I thought I felt an unwanted presence here, but you will not defeat me. I have obtained all the power of the unicorns."

"You have not gained all the unicorn power. Two foals have been born with ten times the power of the last herd, and the ancient charm of power has returned to our land. Right at this moment, the last unicorn has renewed its strength."

"You are wrong! My mighty servant, Uniscale, has stolen the formula from your herd. They are doomed."

With those last words, Aaron and The Hunter charged toward each other with a clash of swords; they swiped at each other with the loud ringing of the swords as they continued to gain ground back and forth. The Hunter knocked Aaron's sword from his hand, leaving a large gash on Aaron's wrist causing blood to gush from the wound. Aaron rolled away, placing pressure on his wrist. Splendor attacked The Hunter from behind causing him to be caught off guard with a slash on his head. The horns on his chest glowed and from where the gash on his head was a large horn grew. Splendor flew out of reach of the horn and swooped down, picking Aaron up and flying into the forest.

Aaron grabbed everberries from his pouch with his other arm. He threw them into his mouth, chewed, swallowed, and soon his wrist was healed.

The Hunter chased after them. As they reached the forest edge, Omon dove between The Hunter and Aaron, spewing fire at The Hunter, hoping to harm him. To his dismay, the fire barely burned the scales as a thick coating of ice smothered the fire out. Splendor and Aaron escaped high over the trees, and The Hunter continued to attempt to pursue them into the forest.

The Hunter was then confronted with a painted unicorn covered in a splash of purple and pink with a horn that was aimed straight for his heart. With a shock, he recognized the painted unicorn as Uniscale, only this was Uniscale before he had cursed her. Eyes, red with anger, were charging full speed ahead toward The Hunter. He placed his huge arm up to protect his heart as the razor sharp horn hit him. The arm which was removed immediately regenerated. He grabbed at the horn with his strengthened hand to break it off, but it was as hard as diamonds and couldn't be removed. As blood burst from his hand, he let go allowing his hand to heal itself.

"You traitor! How can you fight with the unicorns! I have cared for you when you were weak and given you new strength."

"I never wanted to join forces with you, but you overpowered me. I will now avenge my family and my tribe. You will pay for all the destruction you have placed upon the unicorn tribes. I am no longer under your power. I have emerged from the hideous creature you created me to be. I am now alive and the power of my ancestors has returned to me ten times greater."

As Uniscale slashed deeply in The Hunter's heart, a high screech escaped from his mouth, but the wound was not fatal, and the horns he wore started glowing and his scales returned to close up the wound. Omon joined the battle with Aaron and Uniscale. The fighting created a cacophony of noise and birds throughout the forest took flight.

Katrina and Starscape headed into the woods to find Lunar and the herd to lead them to the battle. Omon dove from the sky, aiming for The Hunter's eyes, but The Hunter's sword slashed at the dragon's wing that had been repaired. Fortunately, it retained a stronger power like stone, and the sword barely scratched the wing. Omon knocked the sword from The Hunter's grip as Uniscale went for The Hunter's legs, causing him to be knocked off balance. Aaron made another pass by The Hunter, but with no success. The Hunter reached up with his bare hand and knocked Aaron off of Splendor. As Aaron was free falling to the ground, Splendor sent out a brilliant light into The Hunter's eyes. He was blinded temporarily as Omon, Spendor and Aaron dove deep into the nearby forest, nearly crashing down in front of Cindy and the foals who were moving toward The Hunter.

The Hunter moved into the forest where he sent out an icy wind that froze Aaron, Cindy and the foals to the ground. Omon blew a fiery hot shield upon Aaron, Cindy and the foals so that the ice melted into steam. The group hid themselves in the steam, infuriating The Hunter and allowing them to move deeper into the woods to regroup. The two foals and Splendor joined their powers to produce a shield that camouflaged them with their surroundings, so The Hunter couldn't see them.

Uniscale charged into The Hunter knocking him to the ground. She pointed her horn toward his unicorn horn mail trying to knock it from his chest. He rolled away from her, knowing the horns he had stolen were his mighty power, and if it was taken from him he would be weakened. As he rolled away from Uniscale, she pierced his back, causing a great gash across it in exactly the same place where Lunar had injured him from their previous battle many years ago. In that battle, Uniscale had lost. This time, she was determined to not experience the same fate.

The wound ripped open causing a lava like substance to seep out. As it moved across the ground, the trees splintered and sparked, creating a melting of the ground around Uniscale. She jumped high over the melting ground and with the touch of her horn, the lava stopped flowing. Getting back on his feet, The Hunter pursued Uniscale. Using the horn he had grown when Splendor slashed his head, he moved toward Unicale, attempting to slice her neck. Just as he was about to cut her, she was zapped away in a blinding light.

Obsidian saw where Uniscale was and telepathically called her away from The Hunter. In a flash, she arrived in the shield with the others, startled by the sudden move from one spot to the other.

Stunned, The Hunter stood in the woods by himself wondering where everyone had gone. He roared and the terrifying sound shook the trees surrounding him.

Chapter 22

Standing underneath the protective camouflaged bubble, the crowd of allies heard the roar and turned toward the sound. Suddenly Uniscale appeared amongst them.

"How did I get here? However it happened, I am grateful. The Hunter almost slashed my neck. Where are Katrina and Starscape?" Uniscale asked.

"She and Starscape have dashed off to find the rest of the herd and hope to sneak up behind The Hunter to catch him off guard and hopefully with their combined power, they may be able to weaken The Hunter," Amethyst said.

Cindy interrupted, "We cannot attack on our own or in small groups. We need to have a plan and work together to defeat him. Haven't you noticed that each time we battle with him by ourselves or in small groups we are unable to do much damage?"

"How is he so strong and almost indestructible?" Omon queried.

"I would guess it has to do with all the power he has stolen from us unicorns because our horns are very magical and powerful even when they are not attached to us. That is why once our horns are gone, we lose our power and whoever possesses them retains that power," said Uniscale.

Cindy put the pieces together in her mind. "So, if we can get the horns off of The Hunter, he will have less power. So how could we do that?" Cindy pondered out loud.

"If we could get his unicorn horns off his body, he would have less power?" Obsidian said.

"But he also has the power of the Everberry bush that helps his body regenerate," Aaron said.

Now, Uniscale interrupted, "As I was battling with him before I got here, I had reopened the wound that was a scar that Lunar gave him, and it weakened him, but the goo that came out was like lava. As it creeped across the ground, it melted the ground around me. I was able to jump above it using my power to freeze the lava seeping from his wound. But I don't know if it healed or what happened to him after I arrived here."

Cindy heard a voice in her head. "Cindy Where are you? We can see The Hunter, but we do not hear any battle. The Hunter is alone looking around, confused. What happened?" Lunar mindspoke.

"I was just wondering how far away you were from us. I am working on a plan to surround The Hunter. Stay hidden. Are you approaching from the back or front of Hunter?"

"We are behind him right now as long as he doesn't turn around."

"Hold your position. Slowly fan out around him. The goal for everyone is to get the unicorn horns off of The Hunter. That is what is giving him his power. Once we all work together, we should be able to accomplish that goal. The others and I will surprise him by showing ourselves in front of him. Omon and Spendor will use cloaking powers to move above him and attack from the sky. As soon as you see us appear in front of him, slowly close in on him, and aim your powers at his legs as if to cut them off. He should stumble and fall before he can regenerate his broken legs," Cindy explained.

The plan moved forward as expected. The Hunter was like a caged animal. He circled the clearing that he had created with his lava, trying to discern where Uniscale was at this time. He could find no tracks, and the fact that his hunting skills had failed him was making him furious. Fortunately for the large group of allies, who were silently surrounding him, he wasn't looking for an attack, believing that he was the strongest among all of them. Actually, he was the strongest amongst all of them individually, but when they pooled their energy and their talents, he had no chance.

When Cindy, Obsidian, and Amethyst entered the clearing, The Hunter turned toward them and started moving forward menacingly. The two young unicorns crossed horns, looking intently at the ring of unicorn horns around The Hunter's chest. The horns were released from the armor as the foals focused all their power on his chest. The glowing horns that represented so much pain to the tribes clattered to the ground.

Suddenly, Splendor and Omon appeared above The Hunter and Lunar and the herd of unicorns with their newly grown horns appeared behind him. Splendor and Omon sent a blinding flash downward toward The Hunter just as Lunar and the herd pointed their horns toward The Hunter's legs. He continued to move toward Cindy and the foals, just as his legs splintered beneath him. He didn't realize his powers were declining quickly with the loss of his unicorn horn mail. As the horns had dropped to the ground, Katrina, surrounded by a protective light, picked them up off the ground and moved them off the battlefield.

The horns had an icy hot sensation as Katrina collected them; as the pile grew, so did Uniscale, Cindy and Aaron's power. Soon, The Hunter was shrinking, and as the last horn was gathered, Uniscale turned completely into the painted unicorn that she had been prior to her capture, shimmering with a golden light. As she moved closer to the stack of horns which now glowed like pearls, she let out a multicolored breath and each horn turned into a mighty unicorn.

The Hunter had been defeated. A melodious song erupted from the renewed unicorn race, and they celebrated their victory.

Lunar and his herd moved toward the joyous sound and were amazed at all the unicorns surrounding Aaron and the girls. The unicorns were hues and colors of rainbows and earth. Some were bright like a field of wildflowers in the spring, bursting with life and beauty. Some were pure white and others were dapple gray. There were black roans, bays and chestnut ones, sorrel light reddish, yellow and golden ones with white manes. There were even some that had spots like leopards. Some even looked like appaloosas with distinct markings of white across the rump.

The girls were amazed being surrounded by all the brilliant colors of the new unicorns. Their noses were overwhelmed with the scent of lilac as the foals moved closer. It felt like blankets fresh from the dryer warming them as the unicorns surrounded them. Their noses felt like silk as the unicorns nuzzled them with the Shimmering of fresh dew reflecting the light of the sun at the break of day. Overpowered with a peace like none they had ever felt, they were in awe of the beauty that surrounded them and felt wrapped in love and appreciation for how they helped renew the life of the unicorns.

Chapter 23

Gia moved from the pure white unicorns into an array of multicolored ones. Wading through the sea of majestic unicorns over to her friends, she allowed her hands to pass over all the velvety noses of the shimmering unicorns, and she was encircled with an indescribable warmth and joy.

"Where did all these unicorns come from?" Lunar asked.

Starscape ran over to greet Lunar.

"Our mother is alive!"

"What do you mean alive? She was destroyed by The Hunter so long ago," Lunar said

"No, she is here. She was put under a spell that turned her into a scaled unicorn," Starscape said.

"That can't be. I saw him kill her," said Lunar.

"He put a curse on her that turned her against the unicorns."

"Starscape came with us to capture Uniscale. We worked together with our powers to overcome Uniscale and freed her from The Hunter's spell that had bonded her to him," Katrina said. "After Omon recovered the cure for the unicorn horns, he and Gia headed back to camp. That's when her scales fell off, and her white fur transformed into rainbow colors.

"Our mother breathed life back into the horns that The Hunter had taken over the last several years," Starscape explained.

Just as Starscape was done explaining that their mother was alive, she approached Lunar from behind. Lunar felt her presence, turned and nuzzled her nose.

"Mother, I can't believe you are alive. I have missed you so much. I have tried my best to take care of the herd."

"You have done an admirable job. I can tell the power of the herd has grown tremendously. I am so glad you summoned the girls from Aaron's world to help us defeat The Hunter."

"I would like you to meet your grandchildren. Amethyst and Obsidian, come here and meet your grandmother!"

"What majestic children you have."

"Thanks, Mom."

"I didn't know you could bring life from the horns of our ancestors," Starscape said.

"I had forgotten the power I once had. After my scales started to fall off my back, I felt a strong power overcome me with new strength. I was set free and was drawn to the horns not realizing I could breathe life into things that had been destroyed," Morning Song explained.

"We will have to gather the council of unicorns to discuss how to manage all our new brothers and sisters," Lunar said.

"Starscape, you have no horn," Gia said.

"What? I still can communicate and understand everyone. I must not have realized that with all the magic going on around me that my horn has not grown back," Starscape said with a sigh.

With the multitudes of unicorns, Lunar knew it would be hard to all travel together. If they did, they would leave a scar in the areas they would travel through, leaving an ugly path behind them along the lush unicorn valley. When The Hunter had disappeared into the ground after being vanquished, the land had been restored into a lush garden field full of flowers, and he didn't want to cause any damage to the land.

Settling down for the night under the star spangled sky with whispering winds blowing over the field, the unicorns rested. With a peace they hadn't felt in ages, the herd drifted off to sleep.

Lunar, Moonbeam, Starscape, Aaron, Splendor, and Morning Song all knew that somehow they would have to divide the unicorns into different tribes to spread them out and repopulate the world in which they lived. They also wanted to make sure that all the unicorns knew that they were all created equally. No group would be better than any other. They worked together to come up with possible solutions.

Starscape suggested, "What if we spread out to the north, south, east and west?"

"Yes, that's a great idea, but how can we decide who goes which direction?" Lunar said.

Moonbeam suggested that they let the new unicorns choose which direction they wanted to go.

But what if they all want to stay together?" Lunar said.

"I think if they are anything like other creatures, they would prefer to stay by the ones most like themselves. It's sort of hard to feel you belong when you don't look like others in your family groups," Aaron said.

The girls approached and stopped short. "Sorry," said Gia. "It looks like you are in a deep conversation."

"Yes," Aaron said, "but you are welcome to join us. We are trying to figure out how to divide up all of the new unicorns because there are too many to stay in one area."

"Have you looked at how the unicorns are sleeping?" Gia asked.

"No, we have been concerned on how to move forward with so many young unicorns," said Aaron.

"Take a break and look out at the field. They seem to have naturally bonded together with those that are most similar to themselves and bedded down in their own groups," said Katrina.

The leaders peered out over the hill at all the sleeping unicorns which looked like a patchwork quilt carpeting the field.

"Amazing! I would have never thought this would happen," Lunar said.

"Well, that is one problem solved," Starscape said.

"Now we need to select leaders for each group," Morning Song said.

"I am exhausted. I think we should all try and get some rest. It has been a trying last few days," Aaron said.

"Most definitely," Splendor agreed. "Omon and I will keep watch over the herds tonight even though I don't think there is any immediate danger approaching."

"You need your rest too, Lunar. I can watch over the herds tonight with Splendor," Omon said as he took off into the night sky.

Chapter 24

As the sun peeked over the mountains, the herds began to awaken. The unicorns continued to celebrate the peace and enjoyed being with each other. As the day progressed, the unicorns were starting to feel as if they were corralled by an unseen force. As they looked around the field, they also noticed that where they had grazed had practically turned into a dirt desert. Echoing across the valley, a loud voice could be heard.

Aaron said, "Attention! Attention, all unicorns. I have an announcement to make as Guardian of this land and all the animals that reside here. I realize it will be impossible to all stay together as one herd. I have decided to hold a council to decide who the new leaders of each family herd will be. We are pleased that you have chosen your family tribe. We now would like to appoint leaders for each tribe like was done before The Hunter came. We are different tribes, but we understand we need to keep the unity. Once the unity was compromised, evil started to take over our land.

Aaron continued, "I've selected a council to choose leaders for the new herds. I will confirm their choices. We will ask each group to move to the north, south, east, or west with the leader that will be chosen. Once we set leaders, you will go with them. You will want to follow them. If for some reason, you find that you want to live with a different group, you are free to move to that group. We have decided to break the very large herd into smaller groups merely to ensure that everyone will have enough food to eat."

A few unicorns moved around the meadow which was now completely stripped of vegetation.

"Throughout our lifetime, the leaders will meet regularly at every full moon to discuss any matters that need to be addressed. We will plan on having a final night together as we announce our leaders. Since we all have eaten heartily of this meadow, we will spread out to the north of the valley, so we can continue to graze and rest after our harrowing experience. Then, in the morning, we will part and go our separate ways," he finished.

The chosen council included Moonbeam, Lunar, Morning Song, Starscape, Aaron, and Splendor. The girls and the foals were asked to be on the council. Their opinions were valued, but they did not have a vote.

When the council joined together, a myriad of questions were asked, and all needed to be considered before leaders could be chosen.

Splendor said, "How are we going to decide who each leader should be? I think we need to have unicorns who are experienced and know how to lead and protect their charges."

Lunar said, "A leader should always put the safety of his herd ahead of him or herself."

Moonbeam said, "They need to show authority and be able to stay calm in an emergency."

"A good leader needs to be open-minded and to be willing to learn from both young and old alike," said Aaron.

"And include a vote from every herd member if a major choice needs to be made," added Starscape.

"A leader must also be able to withstand and accept criticism with grace and understanding," said Moonbeam.

Splendor added, "A leader needs to teach their charges to be respectful of others and remind them to step into each other's hooves."

Morning Song added, "They need to consider what each member has been through in both the present and the past."

Starscape finished, "And above all, they need to keep the unity in each herd, and they must not shun anyone or think they know everything."

Katrina added, "I believe that Starscape has displayed several of these leadership qualities. He was the one who alerted us to the thief's position and charged in to help. He has made a huge sacrifice of putting everyone else before himself."

Cindy added, "He gave up the chance to become a unicorn again and is now still hornless when he stayed with us instead of going back with Gia and Omon.

"You are right. I am so proud of you, my little brother. You have grown in maturity and have developed many of the key characteristics of a true leader," Lunar said.

"Thanks big brother. I keep forgetting that I am hornless. I still seem capable of the things I did when I did have a horn. I do not know why that is," Starscape said.

Smiling, Morning Song said, "Because your heart has changed. You are able to still have the ability to be a great leader. You're still a unicorn in your heart."

"Thanks Mom, but will the others respect me without a horn, or will one of the others want to take my place?"

"I don't think that will be a problem." Summoning Amethyst and Obsidian near her, she directed them to join their horns together with hers and focus on Starscape's forehead while visualizing a new horn. A new horn started to grow out of his forehead.

Starscape felt a tingling sensation like a popsicle on a hot summer day cooling a dry throat and then a bright light illuminated his horn, and it glowed like fireflies on a summer night.

"What amazing powers my foals have. I would never have dreamed there would be so much power in my little ones," Moonbeam said.

"Has there been such power before in twins born to our herds?" Starscape asked.

Morning Song said, "You and your brother would have had similar powers if you had stayed together in our herd. When twins are born to a chosen mare, they are born stronger and with more power than the twins before, but they must stay close to each other in order to enhance this strong power. Your father didn't want either of you to take over his herd. That is one reason he banished Lunar and me."

"You mean, our father knew that we would be able to overpower him if we stayed together?" Starscape said in amazement.

"Yes, but he was so power hungry, he didn't want to let it go and that was what started the decline of the Starlight herd, which, in turn, caused the rest of the herd to turn against us. That is why unity is the strongest power in the universe. When all work together and use each creature's unique gift to join together to become a cohesive unit, strength for the entire herd is built. As the saying goes, 'a three strand rope is stronger than a single strand by itself.' In other words, as we join and work together as a complete unit, we are strong and cannot be easily broken."

The girls looked at each other sheepishly.

"We didn't work together at first. It was a lot easier when we let each other use their strengths and built upon them," said Cindy.

"You mean, we all need to realize how as we work together in unity that we have become stronger in our gifts and to remember to always work together?" Katrina said.

"I'm sorry Katrina that I didn't think you could change, but all through our journey here, you have learned to look out for others, as well as work together to accomplish great things," Cindy said.

Gia added, "I agree. I am sorry I doubted that you would change."

Obsidian asked, "So, who are the new leaders going to be? Amethyst and I aren't going to be leaders of one of the tribes, are we?"

"Not right now. You are still very young, and you also need to grow into leadership and develop the skills of a leader before you can lead," Moonbeam said.

"Speaking of that, we need to get going on who will lead which group," Aaron said.

"May I volunteer to be the leader of the group that will go to the north near the woods?" Starscape said.

"I would like to lead the group of bright colored unicorns like the rainbow. We could go south," said Morning Song.

Lunar said, "Moonbeam and I will take our herd back to the hidden valley by the Turquoise River, and we will be happy to include the other black and purple unicorns who want to join us, so we can train Obsidian and Amethyst to take over our herd."

"So that would leave Aaron and me to protect and lead the wildflower colored tribe to the field of wildflowers west toward the sea and by Aaron's cottage," Splendor said.

"Aaron, aren't you going to come back with me? I don't want to be without you back home," Cindy said.

Chapter 25

"I have been dead to your world for so long; I don't think it would be advisable for me to live in that world again. Lunar and Morning Song have been my family. I don't want to leave this place."

"But Dad and Mom would be so happy to know you are alive, and maybe if Dad sees you and knows you are alive, he will be able to be set free from his grief...and maybe...just maybe...he would realize I am his child too, and he might even learn to accept me for who I am instead of saying 'If only… Please Aaron, please come back with me, and at least, let them know you are alive."

Gia and Katrina and the foals surrounded her with hugs to help her through this disappointment. As they gathered around, she felt a peace she hadn't felt before.

Morning Song nuzzled Aaron and spoke directly into his mind. "Your father needs to see you to have closure and say farewell to you. He has been grieving too long. I know that once he sees you, he can have peace in knowing you are safe. It needs to be done. Your sister has been so distraught because of your father ignoring her."

Aaron looked over at his sister. He hadn't realized how hurt she had felt without the love of a father. His heart broke as he realized how his death had affected his dad. He walked over to Cindy and hugged her.

"Can we make a compromise? I will come home with you and your friends to visit Mom and Dad. I will then need to come back to this land for this is where I now belong. I will not be able to live in your world, but if ever you want to come visit me, or if Dad and Mom want to see me, they can come to my land and visit me with the charm you have. It will allow you to move between worlds, but only if you choose to do so."

Cindy looked at Aaron with surprise.

"You mean they can visit you?" "I mean they can visit if YOU want to bring them. You have the control in this situation, for the charm will only work in your hand."

Cindy gave Aaron a huge hug, and the two didn't let go of each other for a long time. Brother and sister were connected as one.

The next morning, the herds gathered together to meet their leaders and to divide into four new tribes of unicorns: the Rainbow Tribe, the Woodlands Tribe, the Tribe of the Turquoise River and the Wildflower Meadow Tribe.

Aaron announced, "We have chosen the leaders for each family tribe. Morning Song will lead the newest tribe, the Tribe of the Rainbow. You will be living to the south. You will be known as the Tribe of Renewal because Morning Song is the one who brought new life from the discarded horns that The Hunter took. She is the wisest and the most powerful of the unicorns. She is the mother of Lunar and Starscape. She was cursed by The Hunter but now is alive and strong. She is the giver of life. She also has great wisdom to impart to her herd. She will be a fair and generous leader. She will appoint a co-leader from the Rainbow Tribe to share in the duties of leadership. Step over with her if you have chosen to follow her."

There was general movement among the large group of unicorns as many moved to stand with Morning Song. An array of sparkling hues of the rainbow parted from the large herd and headed to the south of the field. Wherever the unicorns stepped, new vegetation started to grow. As the field was enhanced, the purest colors were birthed into new life.

"Step forward, Starscape," Aaron said.

Gia introduced him. "Starscape has shown great devotion to his family and tribe. He chose to help us save the formula to regenerate all the horns that were removed from the last unicorn herd. He could have returned with Omon and me to place the potion on the unicorns that had lost their horns. Instead, he chose to go with Katrina and Cindy to aid Aaron in battle with The Hunter. By doing so, he sacrificed his opportunity to gain his power back, knowing that he would be a stallion forever. This is Starscape, the humble and brave. He will be leading the Woodland herd, as they travel to and live in the northern forests. He will teach the value of putting others before yourself and to be the warriors of the woods. He will be assisted by Omon the dragon, Defender of the Woodlands. All those who have chosen to be with Starscape may move toward the nothernwoods."

The unicorns the color of the woods swiftly moved to Starscape. Like melted chocolate flowing down a fountain, they merged together and converged near the forest trees. Rising on their hind legs, they gave a mighty victory cry.

"Step forward, Lunar and Moonbeam," Aaron said.

As Lunar and Moonbeam stepped forward, Katrina and Cindy introduced them and the foals. "This family will be the leaders of the Tribe of the Turquoise River Valley. They have been co-leaders of the last unicorn tribe. With the birth of Amethyst and Obsidian, they have been through many challenges as leaders, but still their herd has shown the power of unity and grace and that by working together, you can accomplish great things. They will be the protectors of the Hidden Valley of healing plants. Those from the original herd may join them as they will be heading to the east as well as any who are purple, white or black may join them as well."

They moved toward the center of the field, so everyone could see the new foals and welcome them into the tribe. As the ancient tribe came to the center of the field, sunlight danced across their fur, shimmering like flashes on a lake with dew drops on their horns. A small pond appeared next to where they stood with splashes of light reflecting from the turquoise pond.

Aaron said, "Splendor and I will be taking the Guardianship of the Wildflower herd west toward my cottage near the wildflower fields. As the young ones grow, I will be the Guardian of this land, working with Splendor. We will fly across the lands to make sure our world is safe and secure till the end of time. Come forward and stand with me."

Like flowers blowing on the wind, the young pastel unicorns surrounded Splendor. As they moved across the field, they left flowers wherever they stepped. They bowed their horns to their new leaders in respect for them. A fairy ring appeared around them as dragonflies like fairies fluttered around the unicorn tribes, sprinkling them with bright colored glitter to announce the start of new life on the land.

Aaron looked at all the unicorns of the valley, now standing in groups with their leaders. "I will be leaving temporarily from this world as I return my sister and her friends safely back to their land. I also have some unfinished business to do before I can return to this land. Until I return, Splendor will lead you to your new home and get you settled into life there."

Chapter 26

"Before we part and go our ways, I need to call on your unity power and music to send our new friends—Cindy, Katrina and Gia to their world where I will accompany them on their journey back. I would like you to form a circle around the girls with your horns turned toward us. I need you to summon your magic and sing the unicorn song to send us back into their world," Aaron instructed.

Before Aaron descended down the hill to take his place next to the girls, he took in the wondrous view of a new nation connected by unity, respect, and love. He admired the luster of the multicolored horns reflecting the light, painting the field into a profusion of colors. A melodious song surrounded them as Amethyst, Obsidian, Moonbeam, Starscape and Omon came to the center of the circle to say good-bye. Katrina and Cindy hugged the foals as tears rained down their cheeks. They snuggled close to them, soaking in the sweet scent of buttercups and orange blossoms as they buried their faces into the manes of the foals.

Gia moved over to Moonbeam and Omon. She gave them each a long hug as she felt a strong connection to them. She could feel their appreciation and love for her and the unique connection they had since Gia had assisted them in their healing. She had not realized how using her healing knowledge and power connected her so deeply. Lunar nuzzled each of the girls as they moved into the center of the circle.

As the melodious songs rose louder around the group, the hues of all the unicorns danced around them like the colors shining in the colors shining in the northern lights. The world started to spin like a merry-go-round on a playground. A tingling sensation filled their bodies as they all clasped hands, spinning faster and faster.

The singing faded, and they landed with a thud on the floor. When they recovered from their dizziness, they opened their eyes and saw that they had arrived in Katrina's room at the same time they had left.

Molly was startled from her sleep and awoke with a fierce growl and started to attack Aaron. He calmed her anxiety, and she approached him and then licked his face as a welcome back for she recognized his scent from when he was a little boy who pulled her out of the basket and hugged her close to show his parents he had chosen the pup he wanted.

After the greeting from his dog, he noticed that there were some very different things here that were not in this world when he was last here. He heard a rumbling sound and looked down to see a circular disc moving toward Molly. He tried to get her to move, but she was too busy licking her old friend. When the disc got close to her, it turned and started moving in a different direction. Gia noticed what he was looking at and laughed.

"That's a vacuum cleaner. It's a robot and will clean the carpet and floor continually when no one is here. It must have started working while we were gone and didn't realize we're back. Don't worry. It will go back to its charging station now that it senses that we're here."

"Why isn't Molly afraid of it?" Aaron asked as he watched the robot move into the kitchen of Katrina's apartment in the hotel.

"She's used to it," said Cindy.

"Do you have one at home?"

"No, we didn't have one, and right now, we don't even have a home because of this fire, but I'm not going to worry about that right now," Cindy finished.

Katrina called out, "Alexa, turn on the TV."

Suddenly, a large painting that almost filled one wall changed to a television screen and scenes of a large fire filled the screen. The girls were transfixed by the fire and appeared to be listening about the status of the fire.

Aaron was fascinated by the fact that someone named Alexa had changed the large picture in the frame on the wall to a television that was huge and had every color and more detail than he could ever remember seeing. It now appeared that the photographer was flying in a plane over the fire. It was making him sick. It was much worse than flying on Splendor.

"I don't think I want to watch this television any longer. How about we come up with a plan on meeting Mom and Dad."

"I can't wait to see how excited Mom and Dad will be to see you," Cindy said.

Cindy turned back to her friends. The three of them stood and looked at each other for a moment. It was hard to believe, but it seemed that no time had passed in this world while many days had passed in Unicorn Valley. They would still be together and would share their experiences, but for now, Cindy really had to go. She wasn't sure how long Aaron could stay in this world.

"Bye Gia. Bye Katrina. I will come back later and tell you how it went."

"Cindy, stop. Don't you think you should wait a little bit longer before finding your parents? Remember, we just left our parents to eat to come up here," Gia said. "We first took Molly for a walk for about twenty minutes before we came to Katrina's room."

"Ummm, I may need to change out of my unusual clothes before I... we see Mom and Dad, as I'm pretty sure these clothes would make me stand out."

"I can let you borrow some of my dad's clothes. You are about the same size he is," Katrina said.

"Thanks, that would be great," said Aaron.

The two walked into her parents' room, and then Katrina came out and shut the door.

"Come on already. I want to see how excited Dad will be to see you," Cindy called.

"Slow down, Cindy. Have you thought through how they will react to seeing the son they thought was dead, all grown up?" Gia questioned.

"I am sure they will be pleased to know he is alive and well," Cindy said.

Aaron came out of the bedroom. Except for his long hair and moccasin-like shoes, he looked like everyone else in the hotel. He was a little disheveled, as if he had left his home in a hurry, but he was so muscular and handsome, most people wouldn't have noticed or cared. Many of the people in the hotel had left their homes in a hurry and were disheveled, so he fit right in with the group.

"It was nice meeting you girls. I really enjoyed the time we spent working together," Aaron said as he attached Molly's leash to her harness.

Calling Molly to come join them, Aaron and Cindy stepped out onto the third floor and headed for the stairs.

As they exited the stairwell, Cindy's parents were just walking out of the lobby dining area and saw Cindy and Molly with a stranger. They paused for a moment and looked at the two. They were deep in conversation and Molly, who was very protective of Cindy, was walking peacefully between the two of them. When they paused for a moment, continuing to talk, Molly reached up and licked the stranger's hand. That motion above everything else, told Alex and Sandy that this tall young man was not a threat. He reached down and scratched behind Molly's ears, and the dog leaned into his leg.

The two shocked parents looked at each other.

"Molly doesn't usually do that to strangers," said Sandy.

"I know. It's almost as if she knows this young man," said Alex. "He does look familiar."

The two young people spied their parents standing in the lobby looking perplexed and approached them.

"Hi, Mom and Dad," Cindy said.

Her parents looked at their normally fastidious daughter who looked as if she hadn't had a shower in ten days.

"What did you, Gia and Katrina get into in the last thirty minutes?" asked her mother.

"You look like you've been on a week-long camping trip," said her dad, "and you kind of smell like it, too."

Aaron and Cindy looked at each other and burst into laughter.

Cindy said, "I have a great story to tell you, but first, I need to introduce to someone that you actually know. Take a look at him. See if you recognize him."

Her parents looked at each other, shook their heads and looked back at their daughter.

"Come on, Cindy. Is this Katrina's brother from college?"

"Nope. Katrina doesn't have a brother, but I do. Come and look closer," Cindy said.

Her parents looked more closely, squinting at the tall young man. When he smiled, Alex ran over and hugged him. He had immediately recognized Aaron by a scar over his left eyebrow from when he fell off the swing and had to get stitches.

"I felt that you were still alive," his father said, looking his son over carefully. "How on earth did you get to be so tall?"

"I was on a different plane of earth. Remember the time I said I went to the land of unicorns and dragons? I really was there, and Cindy used the charm I used to travel there. The land has been in danger for many years, and Lunar had to summon Cindy and her friends to help us defeat The Hunter and to help the unicorns grow in unity. But I have to return. I don't belong in this world anymore, and I need to return to my kingdom," Aaron finished in a rush.

Sandy hadn't said one word to her son. She seemed to be in a trance, and then the dam burst, and she asked, "How are you still alive? We buried you in the cemetery. How did Cindy find you? How did you find Cindy?"

Aaron reached over and pulled his mother into his arms. "I don't know how all of it works. Just know that I have been safe and raised by loving parents, although they are very different from you and Dad. As I said, I have to return to the land very soon for there is much work to be done there."

"Can you at least stay for a few days with us before you return to your kingdom?" Sandy asked.

"No, I will need to leave soon," Aaron replied.

"Can you at least visit for a couple of hours? We have just lost our home to the wildfires, and we sure could use some joy in knowing that you are alive, and we want to hear about your adventures in the world of unicorns and dragons."

"Yes, I can spend a little time here."

Walking to their hotel room as a family was a joyous event. They went to the room excited to hear of the adventures. They sat around in the living area of their room listening to the story of how Cindy was united with her brother, and how Cindy and her friends learned to work together and to value each person's gifts. Cindy noticed that her stuffed unicorn that had been white with a rainbow mane now mirrored the colors of Obsidian, her guardian unicorn.

After a while, Aaron explained to his family that he needed to return to his kingdom.

"It's been four days according to unicorn time, and I need to get back and help organize the land. If you ever want to see my kingdom, you are more than welcome. Cindy has the charm, and only she has the power to bring you to see me. She is a very important girl. I'm proud to call her my sister. The citizens of my land are also proud to call her friend, and she's welcome any time. We all love her very much!" He reached over and gave Cindy a big hug.

Then, with more hugs and tears, he vanished and went to his kingdom.

After he had gone, Cindy's father said, "I am extremely proud of you for being so brave and strong in the battle against The Hunter. I am very sorry that I didn't realize how hard it has been for you. I ask that you forgive me. I want to spend more time with you and be there for you when life gets difficult. I want to get to know you so much better in the coming years."

"I forgive you, Dad. I have always wanted you to take me fishing, teach me woodworking and building just like you would have done with Aaron."

"Tomorrow we can check out a fishing store and get what we need to fish, and I will check the computer to see if there are any lakes or rivers around here where we can fish."

"Thank you, Dad. I am going to have so much fun spending time with you."

"First though, you desperately need to take a shower. Aaron smelled masculine in his clean clothes, but you, my dear daughter, stink."

Chapter 27

After her shower, Cindy called Gia and Katrina and invited them to meet her at the park nearby because she wanted to share with them how things went with her parents meeting Aaron.

Arriving at the park about ten minutes later, the girls met with excitement and anticipation of how things went for Cindy and Aaron.

Katrina asked, "So what happened?"

"At first my parents weren't sure what to think. They were confused because Molly doesn't take well to strangers. But when they came out, they noticed Molly was acting like she knew this young man. My dad thought he recognized the scar on Aaron's eyebrow from where he had gotten stitches from when he fell off the swing. Once they got closer, they realized it was Aaron, and Mom wanted him to stay for awhile, but he knew he needed to get back to his land. He was happy to see our parents, but he was also uncomfortable because he didn't like being closed in. He really missed being in the open. After he left, my dad asked for my forgiveness, and he is super excited about getting to know me."

Did Aaron leave my dad's clothes? He wondered about Aaron's woodland garb when he came home. Apparently, I gave Aaron one of his favorite shirts. I'm kind of in trouble."

Cindy laughed. "Nope. I'm not sure how much you want to tell your parents, but right now, your dad's shirt is in the land of the unicorns."

Katrina said, "I haven't decided how much to tell them. What do you think, Gia?"

There was no response from Gia.

Katrina repeated, "Gia. What do you think? How much are you going to tell your mom?"

"Sorry, I was drifting off thinking of the adventure we had and wondering when we can go back and visit again. What was the question again?"

"Are you going to tell your mom about what happened?"

"No, most likely not. It goes against my practical self. Besides, she has enough stress without having a daughter talking as if dragons and unicorns are real. Maybe we can get together again tomorrow."

Cindy said, "Wait, my dad and I are going to go fishing tomorrow. That is one thing I always wanted to do with my dad. It will be a great time to get to know him better, and I can tell him all about me."

"How great! It will be fun to see you develop a better relationship with your dad," Gia said. "Hey, I have an odd question for you guys."

"What?" both Katrina and Cindy said at the same time.

Gia said, "When I got to my hotel room, I saw a stuffed dragon that looked exactly like Omon. I felt his warm breath tickling my ear as I held on to him and could also communicate with him, too. And beside him, there was a stuffed unicorn that looked like Moonbeam. Her horn glowed, and I could hear her speak to me."

Katrina said, "My unicorn also changed colors and looks just like Amethyst. I feel like I can communicate with her, too, and she smells like buttercups and orange blossoms."

Cindy said, "Obsidian took over my unicorn. It's totally black now with a golden horn, and you know that look he gets in his eye, just before he would do something outrageous?"

Gia laughed and said, "That same look you get all the time?"

Acknowledgements

I would like to thank my developmental editor, Alice, for the weekly meetings we had as she gave me insight on how to create engaging characters and exciting scenes. She taught me how to bring all five story elements into each chapter.

A big thank you to the "The Write Practice crew" who gave me feedback and deadlines to keep me on track to finish my book and to catch errors in my writing.

I would like to thank my critical friend, Terri Peterson, who helped me to improve the structure of sentences. She asked many questions to get me to think through what I was writing, alerting me to areas of confusion and helping me to clarify what I was saying. I want to thank her for the many hours of reading and rereading my manuscript, so much so that she was dreaming of my story.

I would like to thank my husband, Shawn, and my boys, Taylor and Joshua, for their support as I spent many hours away from my family. I also want to thank my boys for the inspiration they have given me to create my characters and story.

About the Author

Ginger Summers lives in Loveland, Colorado with her husband, two sons, and two dogs. She entertains and inspires children and young adults with her characters who grow while experiencing challenges in life. She has a variety of publications from a short story eBook, Joshua and Samantha's Magical Adventure, to a picture book, Blundering Fishhooks, published in February 2021. Zahara, her first novel, is the story of a girl who lives on her own in the wilderness while working through the grief of losing her parents. Tree House Dragons was published in 2021 as a short chapter book for lower elementary aged children.

When she is not writing, you can find her exploring nature, scrapbooking with friends, and spending time with her family.

Get in touch with her online:

Facebook@Ginger.summers.90

www.authorgingerasummers.com

Please consider leaving Ginger a review on Amazon, at www.amazon.com/author/ssssummersbyginger22.

Reviews help more people get to see and enjoy this book.

Thank you!

www.ingramcontent.com/pod-product-compliance
Lightning Source LLC
LaVergne TN
LVHW020442070526
838199LV00063B/4816